'How are you?'

'I'm fine, Matt,' she ...

'Yes. Pretty good.' He nodded. 'Congratulations on your promotion, by the way.'

'Thanks. And you on yours,' she added after a moment.

He nodded and she thought she detected a sad little smile around his mouth. Then it was gone and there was an awkward silence between them.

'I'll catch up with you later, Louise,' said Matt quickly.

As Louise made her way back to her office, she was surprised to find that her knees were quite weak. It was never going to be easy, that first meeting again between Matt and herself after a year apart; she'd known that. But it was over now—surely now they could simply get on with their jobs and their lives?

Laura MacDonald lives on the Isle of Wight and is married with a grown-up family. She has enjoyed writing fiction since she was a child, and for several years has worked for members of the medical profession, both in pharmacy and in general practice. Her daughter is a nurse and has helped with the research for Laura's medical stories.

Recent titles by the same author:

POLICE DOCTOR
MEDIC ON APPROVAL
THE SURGEON'S DILEMMA
A VERY TENDER PRACTICE
DR PRESTON'S DAUGHTER

UNDER SPECIAL CARE

BY
LAURA MacDONALD

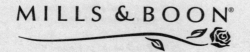

MILLS & BOON®

First published in Great Britain 2003
Harlequin Mills & Boon Limited,
Eton House, 18-24 Paradise Road, Richmond, Surrey TW9 1SR

© Laura MacDonald 2003

ISBN 0 263 83432 8

Set in Times Roman 10½ on 12 pt.
03-0303-49972

Printed and bound in Spain
by Litografia Rosés, S.A., Barcelona

CHAPTER ONE

'HAVE you seen him yet?' Staff Nurse Michelle Burns's face took on an anxious expression.

'No, not yet,' Louise Keating shrugged in what she hoped was an attempt to appear casual, nonchalant even while at the same time she was only too aware that her stomach had churned at the very mention of him.

'Was it a shock when you heard he was coming back?'

'Not really.' Louise shook her head. 'It was always on the cards that he would return to Ellie's after his stint in Scotland.'

'He must be well on his way to his consultancy now,' mused Michelle thoughtfully.

'Yes, I would imagine so.' Louise nodded, wishing her insides would return to normal. If she was like this now, what would she be like when she came face to face with him? And she would, she knew that. There would be no escaping that moment just as she would have to get used to seeing him every day and working alongside him here on the special care baby unit at Ellie's, as it was fondly known, or to give it its correct name, the Eleanor James Memorial Hospital.

'How long is it now since he went to Scotland?' asked Michelle.

'Just over a year,' Louise's reply was terse, almost abrupt and Michelle threw her another anxious glance.

'I thought it must be something like that.' Michelle paused and began sorting through a bundle of folders on the desk. 'Louise…' she began tentatively.

'Yes, Michelle?' Louise raised her eyebrows, somehow anticipating her friend's next question.

'You don't think…I mean…you and Matt…I don't suppose there's a chance…?' She trailed off uncertainly.

'No,' said Louise firmly. 'Absolutely not.'

'Oh, well, never mind… I just wondered, that's all.' Michelle sighed. 'It's just that you seemed…well, I don't know, you seemed so right together somehow and it just seems such a shame that you can't…'

'Michelle, please, just leave it, will you?'

'All right, Louise, I'm sorry.'

'OK,' Louise sighed. 'I know you mean well, but it's all far too late.' She shook her head. 'Now, can we get on with some work? Baby Ruth looks like she needs some attention and here comes Dr Rawlings—she'll be wanting to look at Liam.' She looked up as Senior House Officer Sandie Rawlings hurried onto the ward, her dark hair awry and her white coat flapping.

'Sorry. I'm late. Again,' the doctor said breathlessly. 'It's bedlam down on the children's ward this morning. But I'm here now. I gather there's a problem with Liam Kerrigan?'

'Yes, Louise replied. 'He isn't feeding very well this morning. Oh, and, Sandie, maybe you could stick around for a while because we have a new baby on the way down from Maternity.'

'Sure.' Sandie nodded. 'Do we have any details yet?'

'Caesarean birth, six weeks early. A little boy, I believe. Baby has breathing problems and is jaundiced.'

As Sandie Rawlings moved across the ward to the far side where a nursery nurse was attending to baby Liam Kerrigan, Louise paused and looked around the unit with its mass of high-tech equipment, incubators and cots for eight babies, five of which were occupied that morning with a sixth being prepared at that very moment by another member of her team for the expected new arrival. It gave her a surge of pride and pleasure to know that for part of each day, at least, this was her ward, her domain, and that the post of sister-manager for which she had worked so hard was at last hers. This was her world, this high-tech unit with its tiny, precious patients, most of whom had to fight so valiantly for life itself as the medical teams around them battled to save them. It was a world of extremes: intense happiness and sometimes anguish and despair; full of laughter at times but at others awash with the tears of distraught parents as they struggled to cope with seemingly impossible situations.

Her thoughts were interrupted by the arrival of that morning's newest patient. He arrived in an incubator, accompanied by a midwife from Maternity and his father, who looked shocked and dishevelled, his eyes red-rimmed through lack of sleep, his expression full of anxiety and bewilderment as he attempted to cope with what was happening.

'Good morning, Sister Keating.' The midwife smiled. 'This is Baby Barrett and this is his father, Joe.' The midwife turned to the man at her side. 'Joe, this is Sister Keating—she's in charge of the special care baby unit.'

'Hello, Mr Barrett.' Louise took his hand. 'Welcome to the unit.' She turned to Michelle. 'This is Staff Nurse Burns. She will settle your son into his new surroundings. You can go with her, and then afterwards we'll have a little chat. I'm sure there will be lots of things you will be wanting to ask me.'

Joe Barrett nodded numbly and moved obediently onto the ward after Michelle, unaware that the midwife who until that moment had been his lifeline had left the ward to return to Maternity.

For the next half-hour Louise was occupied with the everyday procedures that comprised the running of the unit—the planning and administration, the delegation of tasks to other members of her team and the endless telephone calls and e-mails to other departments arranging, among other things, visits from members of staff from the consultant paediatricians to heart specialists, from therapists to social workers.

She had just hung up after talking to the theatre sister on Obstetrics when one of her staff nurses popped her head around the door of her office to say that Neil Richardson, the consultant paediatrician, had just arrived on the unit for his morning rounds.

'Right, Nicola, thank you.' Louise rose to her feet, aware that her heart had started to hammer uncomfortably. If the consultant paediatrician had arrived then it stood to reason that his registrar would be with him. She had to get it over with. Maybe once she had got that initial meeting over it wouldn't be so bad. Taking a deep breath, Louise smoothed down her uniform and with her head high stepped out of her office onto the ward.

She saw him immediately, and in spite of the fact that she had prepared herself her heart turned over. He looked exactly the same as he had the last time she had seen him, on that cold March day over a year ago when they had agreed to part and he had walked out of the house and into a waiting taxi.

Just for a moment she had the advantage for she had seen him before he had seen her, and briefly she was able to observe him. He looked well, she had to admit that, fit and athletic-looking with his reddish-blonde hair cropped short, and when at last he turned and his eyes met hers the expression in those green eyes was the same as it had always been, as if he was faintly amused by something.

By this time, however, Neil Richardson had also caught sight of Louise. 'Sister.' Without smiling, he inclined his head in that rather old-fashioned way he had. 'Good morning.'

'Good morning, Mr Richardson.' Louise swallowed, only to find that her mouth was suddenly surprisingly dry. 'Dr Forrester,' she managed to add at last.

'Hello, Louise,' said Matt softly.

For a moment there was silence as if those around them, from Neil Richardson himself to the staff on the unit, were all waiting to see what would happen as she and Matt came face to face again, which was ridiculous really because apart from Michelle and Neil Richardson, hardly anyone else knew. And then, mercifully, it was over as the consultant spoke. 'What do you have for us this morning, Sister Keating?' he asked.

'Liam Kerrigan has been giving a little cause for concern over his feeding,' Louise replied, surprising even herself at how normal she sounded, 'Dr Rawlings has taken a look at him and we have a new addition—Baby Barrett.'

'Ah, yes, I was present at that birth. Shall we take a look at him, Sister?'

'Of course.' Trying to ignore the fact that Matt was watching her, Louise led the way down the ward to where Joe Barrett sat beside his tiny son's incubator. 'Mr Barrett,' she said as they approached, 'this is Mr Richardson, our consultant paediatrician, and his registrar, Dr Forrester. They would like to take a look at your son.'

Joe Barrett looked up and Louise was quick to notice that he had the same bewildered, almost shell-shocked expression on his face that had been there when he had first arrived on the ward.

'Hello again, Mr Barrett.' Neil Richardson nodded. 'We met in Theatre.'

'Did we? I'm sorry I don't remember…' Joe struggled to get to his feet.

'Please, don't get up,' said the consultant in his calm, unhurried way. 'You probably don't remember because I was behind a cap and mask and covered in a green gown at the time. I was the one who whisked your son away.'

'Oh, were you?' Joe frowned. 'My wife…was upset about that…'

'Yes, I'm sure she was,' Neil Richardson agreed. 'Unfortunately, it was unavoidable as he was showing signs of distress.' Taking the notes that Louise passed to him, he studied them for a time then stood looking down at the baby in the incubator who was linked to a heart monitor and who was breathing by means of a respirator. 'We have him stabilised now, Mr Barrett,' he went on after a moment, 'and there is every indication that he will make good progress.'

'Thank you,' mumbled Joe. 'Thank you very much.' He looked exhausted.

Louise's heart went out to him and she resolved to have that chat she had promised sooner rather than later.

They moved on to Liam Kerrigan's incubator where Nursery Nurse Roma Gawn had just unsuccessfully tried to feed him and his mother Lisa was changing his nappy.

Liam had been on the unit for four and a half weeks since his premature birth at thirty-two weeks' gestation. At first he had given grave cause for concern as his birth weight had been very low at a little over two pounds, but each day since he had shown a little improvement.

Louise watched as Neil Richardson carefully and gently examined the baby, doing as little as possible to not disturb him any more than was necessary. It was a scene she watched every day, part of a routine that was to her so commonplace it was as natural as breathing, but today it was different. Today it was as if each of her senses was heightened with an awareness that was almost painful. And what made this even more difficult was that she knew exactly what was responsible, knew precisely what it was that made that day different from any one of those countless others. The cause of her discomfort was the presence of the man who stood opposite her on the far side of Liam's incubator, and as she looked up and their eyes met for the second time that morning she couldn't help wondering whether he felt as she did. Then, averting her gaze, she dismissed the thought. Of course he didn't, she should know better. It would take more than this to faze Matt Forrester.

She had known he was coming, of course she had, had known it was always on the cards that he would return to Ellie's to complete his training and it was pretty inevitable that he would be working here to gain further experience on the special care baby unit since his training in Scotland had been in a neonatal unit. They hadn't actually worked on the same unit before because when he had previously been at Ellie's his work had been on the paediatric ward, while she had been working as a midwife on Maternity before transferring to SCBU. Now, of course, it was different. Now he was Neil Richardson's registrar while she was sister of the unit, so they would have daily contact and would be working together in many situations.

Could she cope with it? she asked herself as they left Liam and moved on to the next baby. Of course she could, she told herself firmly. Besides, she had very little choice and if Matt could cope, so could she.

When the ward round was complete she led the way back to her office where they had a brief case conference on each baby before Neil prepared to leave. It was as Louise was escorting them to the door of the unit that the paediatrician paused to speak to the parents of a baby who was about to be discharged from the unit and Matt turned briefly to her.

'How are you?' he asked quietly.

'I'm fine, Matt,' she replied. 'And you?'

'Yes. Pretty good.' He nodded. 'Congratulations on your promotion, by the way.'

'Thanks. And you on yours,' she added after a moment.

He nodded and she thought she detected a sad little smile around his mouth. Then it was gone and there was an awkward silence between them. As the silence grew, becoming embarrassing, unbearable even, and Louise desperately sought for something to say to end it, Neil took his leave of the couple he was talking to and began walking towards them.

'I'll...I'll catch up with you later, Louise,' said Matt quickly.

There was only time for her to nod in reply then after a brief word to the paediatrician they were gone. Louise clicked the security lock on the doors of the unit behind them and made her way back to her office, surprised to find as she did so that her knees felt quite weak. It was with a decided sense of relief that she sank down onto her chair. It was never going to be easy, that first meeting again between Matt and herself after a year apart, she'd known that, but it was over now so surely they could simply get on with their jobs and their lives?

He'd said he'd catch up with her later. She frowned as she poured herself a badly needed cup of coffee from the machine in her office. What had he meant by that? Probably only tying up the loose ends, she thought as she sipped the coffee, allowing herself to be comforted by its warmth and flavour. And there were loose ends, of course there were. She acknowledged that, just as she knew they had to be dealt with. And probably it was better they were dealt with right away, instead of letting things go on longer than they already had. No doubt, that was all Matt had meant when he'd said he'd catch up with her later. If she was honest, she didn't really want him coming to the house…she somehow doubted she could cope with that. Someone had said he was living in hospital accommodation. Maybe they could meet there to discuss things…or the hospital social club…

She was jolted out of her daydreaming by a tap on her door. 'Come in,' she called, looking up as Nicola Edmunds came in. 'Nicky?'

'Sorry to disturb you, Louise, but were you intending having a word with Mr Barrett?'

'Yes, I was.' Louise nodded.

'Only he seems in a bit of a state.'

'Tell him to come in. I'll see him now.' Louise leaned back in her chair, composing herself and putting all thoughts of Matt firmly from her mind as she prepared to deal with the task in hand.

Joe almost stumbled into her office and sank down onto the chair she indicated. He still looked bewildered, as if what was happening in his world was totally beyond his comprehension.

'I was just having a coffee,' said Louise in as friendly and matter-of-fact a tone as she could. 'Would you like one?'

Joe stared blankly at her as if coffee was the last thing on his mind, but when Louise stood up and moved towards the filter coffee machine he managed a slight nod of his head.

'This must have all come as something of a shock,' said Louise as she poured the coffee and handed him the mug, noticing as she did so that his hands were shaking as he added milk and sugar.

'Yes,' he agreed, 'it did. I'd just come in from work last night and Tracey, my wife, said she wasn't feeling very well. She went to bed and I made her tea, but by late evening she was feeling worse so I rang the doctor.' He gulped as if he found it difficult to go on. 'He came and saw her,' he went on at last, 'and said he was going to admit her because he felt that the baby might be in some sort of trouble. It…he wasn't due for another six weeks… We hadn't decided on a name or anything.'

'This is your first baby isn't, Mr Barrett—Joe?' said Louise gently.

'Yes—that's right.' He nodded and passed a hand over the stubble on his jaw. 'When we got here in the ambulance,' he went on after a moment, 'we were seen by one doctor after another then that Mr…Mr…the one who's been seeing Tracey all along…'

'Mr Finlay?'

'Yes, that's the one.'

'He's the consultant obstetrician,' said Louise.

'Well, he came in and examined her and said he wanted to do an emergency Caesarean. I couldn't believe it. I thought it was much too soon.'

'Caesareans are carried out even earlier than this if they're necessary.'

'Really?' Joe Barrett took a gulp of his coffee. 'I'm amazed. I didn't think the baby would stand a chance. I was there, you know, when he was born—in the theatre. I couldn't really see what was going on—I'm not sure I would have coped if I had been able to—but I sat with Tracey and held her hand.'

'That's good.' Louise nodded. 'It will have meant a lot to your wife to know you were there beside her.'

'I saw the baby when the surgeon lifted him up…then…then they took him straight away… That doctor who was here just now…he…'

'Mr Richardson—yes, he's the consultant paediatrician,' said Louise. 'You had one of the best teams possible with Mr Finlay and Mr Richardson,' she added.

'But…but he…the baby was so small,' said Joe. 'At first, I didn't think…I didn't think he was alive. I didn't think he could possibly be alive. I didn't know what to say to Tracey…then afterwards they said he was in an incubator in Intensive Care… I still don't know quite what to say to Tracey. What if he…? Oh God, what if he…?' With his hands shaking violently now, the coffee slopped over the side of the mug and he set it down on the desk.

Calmly Louise handed him some tissues. As he wiped his hands and she mopped up the coffee on the desk she said, 'There's every chance your son will be fine, you know.'

'Really?' There was no denying the anguish in Joe's eyes as he looked up. 'Do you really mean that or are you just trying to make me feel better?'

'I really mean it.' Louise smiled.

'But he's so small,' said Joe for the second time, as if it was totally beyond him that a baby that small could have any chance of survival.

'He is small, yes,' Louise agreed. 'But we've had smaller babies on this unit, I can assure you. One of our smallest was under two pounds and she came back to see us last week on her first birthday.'

'Was she all right?' Joe stared at her.

'She's a perfectly healthy, beautiful little girl.'

'But…his problems, the doctor said he had problems,' protested Joe. 'I heard him.'

'Yes,' Louise agreed calmly, 'at the moment he does

have some problems but we are doing everything we can to sort out those problems. Now, tell me, did the doctor explain the nature of the problems to you?'

'Yes, I think he did.' Joe nodded slowly then a frown creased his forehead. 'Trouble is, I can't remember what he said.'

'Well, we'll go through them again.' Louise opened a folder on her desk labelled BABY BARRETT. 'To start with,' she went on, 'because baby was so early his lungs aren't quite fully developed so he's having difficulty with his breathing. That's why he is having oxygen—to help him to breathe. He's also attached to a heart monitor so that we can keep an eye on his heartbeat—so far, however, there aren't any indications there's anything wrong with his heart. The other thing is that he's rather jaundiced but that happens with many premature babies. You will find that we will have a phototherapy lamp on him until the jaundice fades.'

'What about feeding him?' asked Joe anxiously.

'He will be fed through a tube.'

'But Tracey wanted to breastfeed him.'

'She still can,' Louise replied. 'She will be able to express her milk and it will then be frozen until it's needed. That way baby will have Tracey's milk from the very start.'

'Well, that's great,' said Joe slowly.

Louise smiled as she realised that during the time he had been in her office Joe had relaxed and seemed much more positive about his son's future than he had when he'd first come in. 'I'll tell you what we'll do,' she said as he finished his coffee. 'As soon as Tracey is feeling a bit better we'll get her into a wheelchair and you can bring her down here to see baby.'

'Really?' Joe looked amazed. 'Can we do that?'

'Of course,' said Louise. 'Baby will be wondering where his mum is and I know for certain that Tracey will be longing to see him.' She stood up. 'In fact, I think I'll see if we can't get this organised now.'

By the time they left the office Joe Barrett was practically beaming.

'What did you give him?' whispered Nicola as he ambled off down the ward to take another look at his son. 'He looks like a different man.'

'It's called hope,' Louise murmured. 'I'm just going to ring through to Postnatal and check on his wife's condition. Then, if all is well, I'd like you to go with Mr Barrett and bring her back here so that they can visit their son together.'

Ten minutes later, after Louise had checked that Tracey had indeed recovered sufficiently to visit her son and, together with Joe, Nicola had departed for the postnatal suite, Louise returned briefly to the mountain of paperwork that seemed to permanently occupy her desk.

She'd barely had a chance to check a couple of forms when Michelle came into the office with the staff holiday rosters.

'I think I've sorted these out now,' she said. 'Jilly is going to swap some shifts while I am away—she wasn't too keen at first but when Nicky pointed out that this *is* my honeymoon after all, she relented.'

'Not long now, Michelle,' said Louise with a smile.

'I know,' said Michelle fearfully. 'For the first time last night I started to feel a bit nervous. I think it was talking to the vicar that did it when he mentioned the rehearsal and I realised just how many people will actually be in church.'

'You'll be fine, Michelle, really you will,' said Louise,

'but while we're on the subject, didn't you say you wanted me for a final fitting?'

'Oh, yes.' Michelle's hand flew to her mouth. 'I almost forgot. Mrs Nesbitt is coming to the house on Wednesday evening—is that all right for you? We've sorted out the little ones but I will need my chief attendant there.'

'Of course, Wednesday's no problem.' Louise paused. 'How's Andy in all this?' she asked a moment later.

'He's been fine.' Michelle grinned. 'But he's starting to get the jitters now.' Then, growing serious again, she said, 'I have to say, though, Louise, he was over the moon when he knew Matt was back.'

'Well, they always were good mates.' Louise shrugged. 'They went right through medical school together.'

'The thing is…' Michelle hesitated. 'He wants…'

'He wants Matt to be at the wedding,' Louise finished the sentence for her. 'Is that it?'

'That's right.' Michelle looked anxious. 'Will that be a problem for you, having him there?'

'Why should it be?' Louise shrugged again. 'I have to get used to him being around again and, let's face it, if I have to work with him on a daily basis I'm sure I can cope with being at the same wedding with him.'

'Isn't it going to be difficult for you, working with him?' asked Michelle curiously.

'I'm not pretending it will be easy,' replied Louise. 'It's just one of those things you have to get on with.'

'Even so, it can't be easy, seeing your ex-husband every day.'

'Actually,' said Louise coolly, 'he isn't my ex-husband yet—we're only separated.'

'Yes, of course.' Michelle frowned. 'But will you be divorcing?'

'Yes, I'm sure that's the next thing on the agenda,'

Louise agreed. Her reply was casual, but even as she spoke and, in spite of the fact that she knew divorce was the next inevitable and logical step, she was aware of a sudden sinking feeling in the pit of her stomach.

CHAPTER TWO

IF ANYONE had asked Louise the same question a week before it probably wouldn't have affected her in the same way. After all, hadn't she become quite accepting, if not resigned in her own mind that divorce would be the next step in the chain of events? Of course she had, she told herself firmly.

So, if that was the case, why was she feeling this way now—as if someone had just kicked her in the stomach?

The answer to that, she was reluctantly forced to accept, was in having seen Matt again. While he had been away, out of her life, it had been relatively easy to get on with things, to hide the sense of failure and disappointment that everything between them had gone so drastically wrong, but seeing him had brought it all flooding back. She had to pull herself together, she knew that. She had a job to do, a very important job in which tiny lives depended on her, and absolutely nothing must be allowed to get in the way of that. With that positive thought uppermost in her mind she made her way out of her office and back onto the ward, and was just in time to see Joe Barrett arrive with Nicola, who was pushing Tracey in a wheelchair.

'Hello, Tracey.' Louise smiled down at the new mother, who looked pale, tired and anxious. 'How are you feeling now?'

'Not too bad.' Tracey turned to look up at Joe then winced with pain as the movement obviously reminded her that she had very recently undergone abdominal surgery. 'I'll feel better when I've seen my baby.'

'Which you are going to do right now,' said Louise.
'Before we do, however, I want to explain to you that baby
is having help with his breathing and he's surrounded by
rather a lot of tubes and equipment. I don't want you to
be alarmed—it's all there to help him.' Turning, she
looked into the ward through the glass partition that separated the babies from anyone else who came onto the unit.
'Come on, Nicola,' she said, 'let's reunite Tracey with her
son.' Together they made their way onto the ward with its
pastel-painted walls adorned with nursery characters, past
the row of cots and incubators to the one that provided a
temporary home for Baby Barrett.

Roma Gawn was tending to him and as they approached
she leaned over the incubator. 'You have some visitors,'
she said to the baby, 'some very important visitors.'

Nicky stopped the wheelchair at the foot of the incubator then manoeuvred it until it was alongside.

'There he is,' said Joe, taking his wife's hand. 'Isn't he
wonderful?'

Baby Barrett lay in the incubator, breathing with the aid
of a respirator, his tiny body with its fine covering of soft
downy hair naked except for a nappy, his head covered
with a soft blue hat and with the various tubes and pads
that monitored his progress attached to his chest and his
arms.

Louise was watching Tracey's face, anticipating her ex-
pressions and her reactions moments before they happened, having witnessed similar ones countless times before—the eagerness, the sudden shock at what she saw
then the helpless tears that filled her eyes.

'He's great, isn't he?' Joe, who had had a little more
time to adjust himself to his son's condition and to all that
was being done for him, crouched down beside Tracey and
took her hand.

'He's…he's so small,' whispered Tracey. 'I…I didn't think he would be that small… Oh, why couldn't he have gone to full term…?' As she spoke the tears spilled over and trickled down her face. Louise reached out to a trolley at the foot of the incubator and, taking a paper tissue from a box, handed it to Tracey.

'Sister said they've had smaller, didn't you, Sister?' Joe's voice was a mixture of excitement and anxiety.

'Yes, we have,' Louise agreed.

'But…look at him.' Tracey's voice was little more than a hoarse whisper. 'Look at his little hands… I've never seen anything so tiny…. And he doesn't look right somehow…' There was slight note of hysteria in her voice now.

It was a voice from behind them that answered her.

'That's because he was so early.' Louise turned and found that, unbeknown to them, Matt had come back onto the ward and was standing behind them as they observed baby Barrett. 'He was quite snug and warm where he was, thinking he had several more weeks to get ready to make his début into the world,' Matt went on. 'And what happens? He has a sudden rude awakening and is catapulted into the harsh light of day when he was least expecting it. Just imagine it. I know how I feel if someone rings the doorbell when I'm still in bed and I'm forced to answer the door unwashed, undressed and unshaven, and as for you ladies, well, I gather it's the end of the world when that happens—aren't I right?' He was looking at Tracey as he spoke, with a quick glance at Nicola thrown in, but Louise knew only too well that it was her to whom he was referring and how he knew how much she hated having to face anyone without having had time to get ready. What he'd said, however, had the desired effect on Tracey who managed a watery smile.

'He's a very handsome lad,' Matt continued. 'Just give

him a day or so to get his act together. I mean, just look at that nose—very noble, I would say.' He glanced at Joe. 'It has to be the Barrett nose. Speaking of which, does he have a name yet?' He looked from Joe to Tracey then back to Joe.

'We haven't really decided, have we?' said Joe. 'Although we do like Oliver,' he added.

'Oliver Barrett,' mused Matt. 'I like that. It has a certain ring to it. Implies success. I would say we have a future banker there or maybe a stockbroker or business tycoon.'

'Am I allowed to hold him?' whispered Tracey.

'It's best not to disturb him too much at the moment,' said Louise. 'But what we can do,' she went on, leaning forward, 'is to open this little window in the side of the incubator so that you can take hold of his hand. See, like this. Go on, Tracey,' she encouraged, 'put your hand through.'

Tentatively Tracey reached out her hand and put it through the side of the incubator. With her forefinger she touched her son's arm and after a moment gently began to stroke it then, moving her finger, she placed it against the palm of his hand, a hand that was little bigger than a ten-pence piece. Immediately the tiny fingers curled and gripped her finger and once again her eyes filled with tears.

'Well, there's no doubting he knows who his mum is,' said Matt with a laugh. 'Dad's turn next.' He grinned at Joe who, as Tracey finally withdrew her hand, repeated the performance, showing equal delight at his son's acknowledgement of him.

'We'll leave you here for a while with baby,' said Louise, 'so that you can all get to know each other.'

'What about feeding him?' asked Tracey suddenly. 'I wanted to feed him myself.'

'And so you shall,' Louise replied. 'I was telling Joe

earlier that we'll show you how to express your milk in due course then you'll be able to help to tube-feed baby.'

They left the Barretts with their baby, and while Nicola went off to assist with another infant Louise and Matt went to Louise's office.

'Was there something you wanted?' she asked. It was rare for the registrar to come back onto the unit after the daily ward round unless he was sent for.

'I wanted to speak to you, Louise,' he said quietly.

'I'm not sure that this is either the time or the place, Matt,' she replied warily. The last thing she wanted was to get into a discussion, or worse, an argument with Matt here on the baby unit.

'No, I know that, but I thought that maybe we could arrange to meet.'

'Well…' She hesitated, wondering quite what he had in mind.

'We have to talk, Louise.'

'Yes,' she agreed. 'We do. I know we do.' She paused. 'Where do you suggest?'

It was his turn to hesitate and she imagined he was going to ask if he could come to the house. If he did, she wasn't quite sure what she would say. It was, after all, still half his. On the other hand she wasn't sure she could cope with him coming there. To have him there again in what after all had once been the home they had shared wouldn't be easy.

'Are Angelo and Maria still at the restaurant?' he asked at last.

'Yes.' She nodded slowly. 'They are still there.'

'Then how about there—later today?'

'All right,' she agreed at last. She wasn't too sure, but they had to meet somewhere. The Italian restaurant had been a favourite haunt once, not just for them but for many of the hospital staff, and it had been through meeting there frequently that they had come to learn about the house almost next door that had come onto the market and had proved to be just what they'd been looking for. But all that, of course, had been in happier times. Much had happened since then and time had moved on.

'You look different,' said Matt suddenly. 'You've lost weight.'

'Have I?' Suddenly she realised he was staring critically at her and to her dismay she felt her cheeks flush.

'Mmm—you look thinner in the face. And your hair is different—I like it,' he said at last, his head on one side as he studied her new jaw-length layered bob with its honey-coloured highlights.

'I didn't think you would,' she heard herself say, as if it still mattered whether he liked it or not. 'You always liked me to wear it long.'

'Yes,' he said softly, his eyes meeting hers, 'I did, didn't I?'

For one wild, awful moment she thought he was going to say something on the lines that he liked to see it spread out on the pillow—it was the sort of thing he might once have said—but to her relief he didn't. Instead, he glanced at the clock. 'I must go,' he said. 'Neil has a clinic he wants me to take. So, what shall we say, four o'clock at Angelo's?'

'Yes, all right.' She nodded, anxious now for him to be gone, aware through the office window that faced the ward that Michelle was casting anxious glances in their direction. 'I'll see you there.'

After he had gone she made her way to the small staff room where, after using the loo and while washing her hands, she looked up, caught sight of her reflection in the mirror above the washbasin and found herself critically surveying it. Matt had said she looked different. Did she? To herself, apart from her change of hairstyle, she looked the same. The same large brown eyes stared back at her, providing that rather unusual contrast—which Matt had often remarked on and had seemed to like so much—to her fair complexion and hair. He'd said she looked thinner— was he being polite? Did he mean older? Had she really changed that much in a year? Had recent circumstances played on her to such an extent that they showed and were etched on her features for all to see?

She frowned slightly at her reflection then told herself that if that was the case then Matt himself had to take his share of responsibility. Things had to change, she knew that, and maybe when they did they would both be free to put the past firmly behind them and get on with their lives.

Louise had a few minutes to spare after finishing her shift before she was due to meet Matt so, after parking her car, she hurried up to the house and inserted her key in the lock. The house was in the middle of a terrace of three, colour-washed in pink with the ones on either side in white and yellow, whilst the terrace itself was sandwiched between the local branch of a well-known high street bank and Angelo's restaurant. It was a tall, narrow house but with unexpected features and characteristics which gave it a charm all of its own. The rear of the houses overlooked the river, its banks at this time of the year dotted with daffodils and early, flame-coloured tulips and fringed with willows whose branches dipped right down into the water.

In the summer one of Louise's greatest pleasures was to sit in the upstairs sitting room, its French doors open onto a small wrought-iron balcony packed with terracotta pots filled with geraniums and watch the brightly coloured barges as they drifted by.

But there was no time for such indulgences now. She barely had time to dump the inevitable pile of paperwork she was forced to bring home in order to keep abreast of her job and to change rapidly into jeans and a sweater before it was time to go and meet Matt. When she was ready she paused for a moment to look around the flat— at the sitting room with its soft golden walls, crimson rugs on the stripped pine floor and tapestry cushions scattered over the two huge sofas, and at the cool cream and white décor of the main bedroom with its pine furniture. Since Matt had left she had slept in the guest room, a smaller room but equally charming in its own style of blues and lilac.

Briefly she found herself remembering how it had been when they had found this house and had spent hours planning the décor—they hadn't even been able to agree on that, she thought ruefully, let alone on those other more fundamental things that went towards building a life together. But she mustn't think about that now. It was the present that was important, the present and the future, not the past. The past, she had come to learn, was another place that she visited at her peril, for it was a place of memories and of what might have been, but the reality of her present situation was vastly different.

With a little sigh and a last glance round Louise ran downstairs and let herself out of the house. It had been a beautiful afternoon and the spring sunshine was still warm on her face, and as she made her way along the pavement to the restaurant she saw people were sitting outside at the tables beneath the dark green awning. There was, however, no sign of Matt so she made her way inside, where she was greeted by Maria Fabiano.

'Ah, Louise, how good to see you!' The Italian woman's dark eyes lit up.

'Hello, Maria.' Louise smiled. She was fond of both Maria and her husband Angelo. 'I need a quiet corner somewhere.'

'Of course.' Maria led the way to a table in a small alcove beneath mock vines laden with grapes and surrounded by frescos of ancient Rome. 'You meeting someone—yes?'

Before Louise had the chance to answer Matt arrived, blinking as he came in out of the sunlight. Then, catching sight of her, he made his way through the restaurant to join her. He'd changed from the suit he wore for work into casual chinos, a sweater and a black bomber jacket.

Maria turned and, seeing him, gave a shriek of delight. 'Matt! It is so good to see you!' she cried, and promptly threw her arms around him.

'Maria, how are you?' Matt grinned and hugged her.

'I am well.' Maria held him at arm's length and looked at him. 'I did not know you were back.' She threw Louise a half-reproachful glance. 'How long you been here?'

'Not long…'

'Angelo! Angelo! See who is here!' Maria cried. Her excitement brought her husband out of the kitchen and further delighted greetings were exchanged between the swarthy Italian and the English doctor.

'I get your usual?' asked Maria, looking at them speculatively at last as Angelo made his way back to the kitchen. 'Cappuccinos for two?'

'Well…' Louise hesitated. She had intended settling for a mineral water.

'Of course,' said Matt with a laugh before Louise could finish. 'How could we come to Angelo's and not have a cappuccino?'

Maria, her black eyes dancing with merriment, bustled

happily away, leaving Matt and Louise to take their seats in the alcove.

He sat for a moment, looking around at his surroundings. 'It's like I haven't been away,' he said after a moment.

'Hardly that.' Louise replied a little more sharply than she had perhaps intended but the warmth of the Fabianos' welcome to Matt had thrown her slightly, although she wasn't sure why. After all, Matt had been as fond of the couple as she had and they of him, so it stood to reason they would be pleased to see each other after such a long time.

'What I meant was that no matter how long you've been away there are some things that never seem to change,' said Matt mildly.

'And others, no doubt, that change beyond all recognition,' she replied.

'Well, yes, quite.' The thought seemed to sober Matt somewhat and by the time Maria reappeared with their coffee he was quite serious.

'So, are you here to stay?' Maria asked, setting the two large steaming cups down before them on the green gingham tablecloth.

'Well, I'm working at Ellie's again, if that's what you mean,' Matt replied without looking at Louise.

It was obvious that wasn't what Maria had meant, that she really wanted to know whether he and Louise were back together again and whether Matt would once again be their neighbour. One look at Louise's face, however, seemed to prevent her from asking more questions. 'I'll leave you now,' she said instead. 'Enjoy your drinks.'

It was probably impossible not to enjoy Angelo's cappuccino, whatever the circumstances, for with its curls of dark chocolate and sprinkle of cinnamon atop a swirl of thick cream, which concealed the rich aromatic coffee beneath, it was sheer, blissful indulgence. On each saucer Maria had placed a chocolate-dipped, almond-flavoured biscuit, just as she had always done on the many occasions in the past when Matt and Louise had frequented the restaurant—in the early, heady days of their relationship when they'd used it as a meeting place and later, when they'd popped in after work or maybe of an evening after a visit to a cinema or a theatre when they'd enjoyed one of Angelo's pizzas.

For a while they sat in silence, nibbling the biscuits and sipping the coffee, until at last Louise spoke.

'We have to talk, Matt,' she said.

'Yes,' he agreed, his sigh almost imperceptible but evident to Louise who knew him so well. 'Yes, I know we do.'

'Have you approached a solicitor yet?' she asked.

'No,' he said quickly. 'Have you?'

She shook her head. 'No. I wasn't too sure how we go about this but I understand we can get a quick, no-fault divorce citing irretrievable differences as the reason for the breakup.'

Matt nodded. 'Yes, that's my understanding of it as well. But...'

'But what?' She had the cup halfway to her lips but she paused staring at him over its rim.

'Are we sure this is what we should do?'

'Well...' she frowned. 'We've been separated for over a year now and the last time we spoke on the phone I thought we both agreed it was the next logical step.' She lowered the cup. 'Didn't we?' she asked at last.

'Yes.' He nodded. 'Yes, we did.'

'Well, then...'

'I know. It's just that it seems so...'

'So what?' Carefully she set her cup back in its saucer.

'So final somehow.'

'Well, yes, it would be. It is. But I don't think either of us want to be simply separated forever—do we?'

'No, I guess not.' Miserably Matt shook his head.

'We have to sort it out, Matt,' she said at last, but more gently this time. 'We couldn't have gone on the way we were—all those rows...'

'I know,' he admitted ruefully. 'It did get pretty hairy, didn't it?'

'You could say that. I think we more than proved that we couldn't live together any longer—speaking of which brings me to the house.'

'The house?' He threw her a quick look.

'We have to sort something out where the house is concerned.'

'The mortgage payments are OK?' He looked faintly startled.

'Oh, yes, they're fine,' she said quickly. 'But that's the whole point. You are still paying...'

He shrugged. 'It's my responsibility as much as yours.'

'Maybe, but the fact of the matter is that I'm still living there and you are living in grotty hospital accommodation.'

'I wouldn't call it grotty exactly,' he protested mildly. 'Basic maybe, but not grotty.'

'All right, perhaps that was a bit of an exaggeration,' she agreed, 'maybe soulless would be better. What I'm saying is that the house has risen considerably in value since we bought it so there isn't even the possibility of me being able to buy you out.'

'Had you considered that?' He raised questioning eyebrows.

'I did wonder,' she admitted, looking quickly away, suddenly unable to meet his gaze.

'But—' he began.

'No, let me finish, Matt,' she said, swiftly pulling herself together. 'The way I see it, the house has to be sold and the proceeds split between us, then you would be in the position to take up another mortgage if you wanted and buy somewhere else to live.'

'And what about you?' His eyes narrowed slightly.

'Well, presumably I could do the same. I dare say it would only be a flat, with the way prices have rocketed around here, but—'

'Alternatively, I suppose I could buy *you* out,' he said, interrupting her as he drained his cup.

'What?' she stared at him. For some reason the thought had never even crossed her mind, but now that he had mentioned it, it did seem feasible, feasible and somehow at the same time deeply disturbing. The idea of Matt living in the house without her, or with someone else, was something she didn't even want to think about, which really was rather unfair in view of the fact that she had been living there alone for the last year and had even considered buying him out herself.

'It might be a solution,' he said thoughtfully. 'I like the house, always did, and it's handy for work.'

'Well, yes,' she agreed uncertainly at last, 'I suppose it is. On the other hand,' she went on after a moment, more positively this time, 'I thought it might be better for us both if we were to make a completely fresh start.'

'You said you'd considered buying me out,' he protested mildly. 'Presumably you would have carried on living there.'

'Matt…' Louise took a deep breath. 'Let's not argue about this. We've only been together for half an hour…'

'OK.' He held up his hands, the gesture submissive.

They were silent for a while then, making a huge effort to keep her voice calm Louise spoke. 'So how was Scotland?' she said at last.

'Yes, it was…OK.' He shrugged. 'A means to an end really—it simply meant completing the next phase of my training.'

'Of course, the next step on the career ladder.'

He threw her a quick glance as if he suspected her of mockery or at the very least facetiousness, but her expression gave away nothing of her feelings. 'You haven't done so badly either,' he said. 'You've got where you wanted to be.'

'Yes,' she agreed slowly, 'I have.'

'I've still got a way to go yet to reach my goal.'

'But you'll get there,' she said. 'There was never any doubt of that.' They sat in silence again, aware of the faint clatter of dishes from the kitchen and the hum of conversation from other diners.

'So where do we go from here?' he asked at last. 'The solicitors?'

'I guess so.' She nodded.

'May I make a suggestion?' he asked tentatively.

'Of course.'

'I was just wondering whether it might be an idea to delay starting proceedings until after Michelle's and Andy's wedding?'

'What do you mean?' She stared at him.

'Well, somehow it hardly seems appropriate that we should be ending our marriage at the precise time that our friends are starting theirs.'

'All right.' She nodded slowly, seeing the sense behind Matt's reasoning. 'That's probably a good idea.'

'Andy tells me you are to be Michelle's attendant.' He turned his head to look at her.

'That's right.' Once again she felt her cheeks grow red under his gaze.

'Sounds like it's going to be a posh affair from what he was saying.'

She nodded. 'Yes, the works…ceremony in the big parish church, reception in a marquee at Michelle's parents' home, honeymoon in the Caribbean…'

'Not like ours, then?' That look of amusement was back in his eyes and Louise felt her lips twitch in spite of herself.

'No,' she agreed wryly, 'not a bit like ours.'

CHAPTER THREE

THEY had met at Angelo's. Louise had seen Matt before, of course, in and around the hospital but they had never actually spoken or been introduced, what with his work being on the paediatric unit and hers as a midwife on Maternity. Angelo's had long been a meeting place for members of staff from Ellie's and one blustery Sunday afternoon in late October two and a half years previously Louise had gone there at the end of her shift, together with Michelle and a crowd of the others. It had been while they'd been sitting there, sipping coffee and gossiping, that Andy Steane had come in with a group of his colleagues. A lot of moving up and shuffling around had followed, and somehow Louise had found herself sitting next to the SHO from Paediatrics.

'Hello,' he said with that devastatingly sexy smile she came to know so well, 'I don't believe we've met.'

'No,' she said, 'I don't believe we have.'

'Matt Forrester—Paediatrics.' He held out his hand.

'Louise Keating—Maternity.' She found her hand encased in a warm friendly grip.

'What are you drinking?' He peered into her cup.

'Cappuccino—it's out of this world.'

And that was the start of it really. They met a couple more times at Angelo's with the crowd and then he asked her out for a meal—not to Angelo's this time but to a little French bistro on the other side of town. 'I thought this might give us a chance to talk,' he said. 'The others are great, but...'

She agreed. She knew exactly what he meant, realising by this time that they both wanted to get to know each other rather better than their usual meetings allowed.

She learnt that his family home had been in Berkshire but that both his parents were dead. 'I have two sisters,' he said, 'both much older than me. I was either an after-thought or a terrible mistake but, whatever, by the time I was born my mother was in her forties and my father was over fifty.'

'Was he a doctor—your father?' Louise could clearly remember gazing at Matt's profile as she'd asked the question and wondering if the strong lines of nose and jaw were a family resemblance. 'Are you following a family tradition?'

'Yes and no,' he'd replied, obviously happy to talk about his family. 'It was an uncle, my mother's brother, who was the doctor. My father was a clergyman, firm and kind but with, well, impossibly high standards.' He paused as if reflecting then had looked at Louise. 'What about your family?'

'My parents are retired farmers and they live in Dorset,' she'd replied. 'I have one brother—he's married with two children and he lives in France,'

'So where are you heading career-wise?' he'd asked a little later in the evening.

'My own ward, sister-manager, I hope,' she'd admitted.

'On Obstetrics?'

'No.' She'd hesitated, unsure about even voicing what she'd really wanted just in case by doing so it somehow would have prevented it happening.

'Go on,' he'd urged.

'I'd like the special care baby unit,' she'd confessed. 'Trouble is, jobs don't seem to come up there very often.'

'Would you be prepared to move?'

'Maybe. Although I have to say I am very happy here at Ellie's. It's where I did my training—it's where my friends are.'

'That's not always a good enough reason to stand in the way of your career.'

'No, I suppose not. How about you?' she went on after a moment. 'What are your plans?'

'Oh, I won't settle for less than consultant paediatrician specialising in neonatology.' Matt was very firm about that, very sure of himself.

'So we're both drawn towards baby care?'

He grinned. 'I guess so. I have to go to another unit soon for the next stage of my training.'

'Oh, really?' She was aware of a stab of disappointment. Was she getting to know him better, only to have him move and probably out of her life? 'And where is that?' She tried to sound interested but not too interested—she didn't want him thinking it mattered too much.

'There are a couple of possibilities—one in Edinburgh and the other down in Cardiff. It just depends which one has a vacancy when I finish the course I'm on at present.'

He took her home that night to the flat she shared with Michelle and she asked him in. Michelle was out. Louise made coffee and they sat talking until nearly midnight when Michelle returned with Andy Steane and the four of them sat on for nearly an hour, perfectly at ease in one another's company.

In the end Matt had to make a move and Louise went down to the front door with him, leaving Michelle and Andy alone.

'It's been a lovely evening, Matt, thank you,' she said.

'Can I see you again?' He looked down into her eyes.

'Oh, yes.' Her pulse was racing and as he lowered his

head she lifted her face to his. His kiss was light but warm and with an edge of excitement that left her wanting more.

After that night they began seeing each other regularly and now, if she was honest, she would have to say that the attraction had been there between them right from the start. Within a very short time she'd known she was falling in love with him.

It was hard to believe that now they were on the brink of divorce.

'I'm sorry, Julie, Russell, but your baby is very poorly.' It was two days later and Louise, sitting in her office, felt her heart go out to the young couple opposite her.

'Can't anything be done?' asked Russell Masters, his face grey with worry and fatigue.

'We are doing everything we can,' said Louise gently. 'Mr Richardson and Dr Forrester are with her at this very moment.'

'I want her to be christened,' said Julie Fox. She seemed the calmer of the two in spite of the fact that she had only given birth the previous day.

'We can certainly arrange that for you,' Louise replied. 'I'll contact the Reverend Mike Collard, who is the hospital chaplain, and he will arrange a time.'

At that moment Neil Richardson and Matt came into the office. 'Mr Masters, Miss Fox.' The consultant came straight to the point. 'I've examined your daughter again and I'm going to make arrangements for her to see the cardiologist.'

'What does that mean?' Russell looked bewildered.

'There's a problem with her heart, isn't there?' Julie looked from Neil to Matt then almost pleadingly at Louise.

It was the consultant who replied. 'I'm afraid it very

much looks that way,' he said. 'But that isn't to say that nothing can be done. We have a first-class cardiology team here at Ellie's.'

'What's happening?' asked Michelle a little later after Neil and Matt had left the unit and the concerned parents were keeping vigil beside the incubator that housed their tiny daughter.

'Mr Green is on his way down to see Baby Gabrielle,' said Louise, replacing the phone receiver on her desk. 'It looks like she has a hole in her heart.'

'Poor little mite,' said Michelle. 'Did I hear Julie say something about having her baptised?'

'Yes.' Louise nodded. 'That's my next job. I must get hold of Mike and see when he can come in. No doubt, Julie and Russell will want some of their family here.'

'If she's to have surgery they'll want it to be before that,' said Michelle, looking at them through the window onto the ward.

'Absolutely. That's why I need to arrange something with Mike now. If Mr Green intends operating, I would imagine it will be pretty soon.' Louise picked up the phone again and dialled the chaplain's number. He answered on the third ring.

'Hello, Mike,' she said, 'it's Louise Keating here.'

'Louise, hello, how can I help you?' His voice was big, warm and friendly, just like Mike himself.

'We have a little babe here, Mike, who's very poorly, possibly facing surgery, and her parents would like her baptised.'

'Of course,' Mike replied. 'I'm just taking communion down to a lady on the medical ward. After that I'll come along and talk to the parents.'

Mr Green and his registrar arrived first and, after examining Baby Gabrielle and studying her test results, the consultant announced that he intended operating later that day.

'Will you be able to help her?' asked Julie, her eyes full of tears.

'I will do everything in my power,' the cardiologist replied.

Mike Collard arrived on the unit as the cardiologist left, and Louise showed him straight into her office to meet Julie and Russell. 'I'll leave you to talk for a little while,' she said. 'In the meantime, I'll organise some tea.' Mike, she knew, was a great tea-drinker and had never to her knowledge been known to refuse a cup.

After despatching Gina, the ward clerk, to the unit's tiny kitchen to brew the tea, Louise went back onto the ward to check on Baby Gabrielle. Roma and Michelle were tending to the baby, gently cleansing her and dressing her in a soft white nightgown.

'Is she going to be all right?' asked Tracey, watching anxiously from her seat beside baby Oliver.

'We certainly hope so,' Louise relied with a bright, positive smile.

'Well, she certainly will be if you staff have anything to do with it,' said Lisa Kerrigan from further down the ward. 'Look what you've done for Liam. When he was born we feared for his life, and just look at him now!' As if to reinforce her words, she turned and looked at the incubator that housed Liam. The baby was awake and appeared to be staring intently up at the brightly coloured mobile of fishes that rotated slowly above his cot.

'Is everything all right?' asked Louise as she reached Gabrielle's incubator.

'She's a poorly little girl,' said Roma, gently smoothing the soft down on the baby's head.

'Is she to have surgery?' asked Michelle, her gaze meeting Louise's over the incubator.

'Yes.' Louise nodded. 'Mr Green is going to operate later today.'

By the time Julie and Russell emerged from Louise's office with Mike it had been decided that Gabrielle would be baptised on the unit at two o'clock that afternoon. Julie phoned her mother and Russell's parents who said they would come to the hospital immediately. 'Will you still be on duty, Sister Keating?' asked Julie anxiously as she finished making her calls.

'No,' Louise replied. 'My shift will be over by then.' As Julie's face fell she added, 'But I shall stay on if you would like me to.'

'Oh, yes. Yes, please. We would like that, wouldn't we, Russell?' Julie turned to her partner.

'Yes,' he agreed, 'we would really appreciate that, Sister.'

When her shift was over Louise handed over to her fellow sister, Martine Lane. 'I think I'll go to the canteen and grab a bite to eat,' she said, 'Then, if it's all right with you, Martine I'll come back for Gabrielle's christening.'

It was crowded in the staff canteen and as Louise stood for a moment with her tray, looking around, out of the corner of her eye she saw someone stand up. Turning quickly to see if the person was vacating a table, she found instead that it was Matt and, far from vacating a table, he was beckoning for her to join him. Briefly she was aware of that curious little feeling somewhere between her heart and her stomach which she seemed to experience whenever she unexpectedly caught sight of Matt, then slowly she made her way across the canteen to join him.

'I didn't expect to see you in here,' he said. 'I thought you would be high-tailing it home at this time of day.'

'I'm killing time,' she said, sitting down and peeling back the plastic covering on her packet of sandwiches. 'Mike is going to baptise Baby Gabrielle at two o'clock and I promised Julie and Russell that I would be there.'

'Two o'clock, you say?' Matt looked at his watch. 'I wonder if I could get there.'

'I'm sure they'd appreciate it,' said Louise.

'It's just that I was present at her birth. I have to say I didn't think she was going to survive then...and, well, you know what it's like.' Matt shrugged.

'Yes.' Louise nodded. 'I know what it's like. You find yourself getting involved even though we know it's the one thing we shouldn't do.'

They were silent for a moment, Louise eating her sandwich and Matt finishing his coffee, then as Matt replaced the cup in the saucer he spoke. 'I was thinking,' he said, 'what we were saying about the house and all that...'

'Yes?' she said quickly, too quickly really.

'Well, I've still got quite a lot of gear there.'

She nodded. There had been no time when he had left for him to pack up all his belongings. Besides, he had been going to Scotland apparently to rent a bedsit for a year.

'I suppose I'd better come round some time and sort things out.'

'Have you got much room?' she said. 'Where you're staying now, I mean?'

'No, not really.' Matt shook his head.

'In that case, it might be a good idea to leave things where they are,' she said. 'Until after the house is sold, that is,' she added hurriedly, 'and you have somewhere more permanent.' Louise paused, for some reason suddenly very aware of him and his closeness to her in the restricted space behind the canteen table. 'Unless, of c-c-course,' she found herself saying, hurrying again now, gabbling almost as she tripped over her words, 'there's anything there you want…you need.'

'No, I don't think so.' He frowned. 'If I'm honest, I've a job to remember exactly what is there—just books and CDs, I think, that sort of thing…'

'There are some clothes,' she said. 'Your good suit and your leather coat…you left that.'

'I know,' he said ruefully. 'I could have done with that in Scotland. I had to buy another.'

It seemed strange to be sitting there in the staff canteen, talking about such personal details with all the hustle and bustle of their staff colleagues around them.

'Well,' he said after a moment, 'maybe I'll call in some time to pick up the clothes and leave the other things, like you say, until later—if that's all right with you?' he added questioningly, raising his eyebrows.

'Yes, of course,' she agreed. How could she refuse so simple a request? But in spite of that she was still very wary of him coming to the house. It was one thing working alongside him and talking to him, even meeting at Angelo's, although, heaven knew, that had been bad enough when it came to stirring up emotions, but having him right there in the very home they had set up together and had once shared, well, that was something else entirely.

'How are your parents?' he asked suddenly, unexpectedly.

She stared at him for a moment, still thrown by the disruptive nature of her thoughts. 'My parents…?' she echoed weakly.

'Yes. Are they well? Your mum wasn't too good at one time, was she?'

'No, she wasn't,' she replied at last as she struggled to pull herself together. 'She had one or two angina attacks, but they seem to have things under control now, thankfully.'

'And your dad?'

'Well, Dad's still Dad.' She smiled and gave a little shrug. 'Yes, he's very well,' she added.

'I miss our chats,' said Matt. 'I never knew anyone who had the capacity for putting the world to rights so much as your dad.'

Louise swallowed. How could she say that her parents also missed Matt, how her mother adored him and how desperately upset they had both been when she and Matt had parted?

'But why?' Her mother had said at the time, obviously bewildered. 'I simply don't understand.'

'It's for the best, Mum,' Louise had said, exhausted and reluctant to go into too much detail.

'Best for whom?' her mother had asked.

'For us both.'

'I really don't see that…'

'Mum, please, just leave it,' she'd said wearily. 'Can we just say that we shouldn't have got married in the first place, that it was all a terrible mistake.'

'I must slip back to Paediatrics.' Louise was jolted back to the present by Matt who finished his coffee and rose to his feet. 'But I'll do my best to get down to Special Care at two.' He smiled, that intimate smile that had once meant so much to her, then she watched him walk away.

She sat for a while toying with the remains of her lunch, wondering if perhaps after all working alongside Matt was going to be more of a problem than she had at first thought. But there was no alternative. She had worked long and hard for her job, just as he had for his, and it was inconceivable that either of them would be prepared to look for another position, which meant that they simply had to accept the situation and get on with their lives as best they could. There was no doubt it would be easier once they were divorced, the house was sold and they had both found somewhere different to live, somewhere that held no memories for either of them. But now, of course, they had both agreed to wait until after Michelle's and Andy's wedding so in the meantime it seemed they would just have to make the best of a difficult situation.

The preparations for Michelle's wedding were in full swing, with the final dress fittings arranged for that very evening and the stag and hen nights scheduled to take place at the weekend.

'But that's a whole week before the wedding,' Nicky had protested when Michelle had told them all.

'Absolutely,' Michelle had replied firmly. 'That's exactly the way I want it. I don't want any hangovers at the altar, neither do I want a wrecked bridegroom or one who doesn't turn up at all because his mates have put him on a train to Aberdeen or somewhere.'

Louise smiled to herself as she recalled how emphatic her friend had been. The wedding was certainly creeping up fast, she thought with a little sigh as she drained her glass of orange juice and stood up. But before then she had a christening to attend.

When she arrived back on SCBU it was to find that Julie's mother and Russell's parents had arrived, and within moments Matt also put in an appearance. They all congregated in the relatives' room where for a while emotions ran high and there were many tears as the seriousness of Baby Gabrielle's condition became evident to her family for the first time. The friends of the couple who had agreed to be godparents had been unable to reach the hospital in time for the ceremony. 'So we wondered,' said

Julie, looking from Louise to Matt, 'whether the two of you would stand proxy for them.'

'Of course,' said Louise, not daring to look at Matt.

'We would be honoured.' There was a catch in Matt's voice as he answered.

Moments later they left the relatives' room, and with Matt wheeling the incubator they all made their way to the small, quiet room at the back of the unit which served as a chapel where, beneath a simple, deep blue stained-glass window depicting a white dove, the Reverend Mike Collard had set up an altar, lit candles on either side of a crucifix and had poured holy water into a porcelain bowl.

Julie's mother had brought a shawl of delicate white lace which, she explained, was a family heirloom. 'Are we able to take her out of the incubator?' she asked fearfully, gazing down at her granddaughter.

It was Matt who replied. 'Of course,' he said, and, reaching inside the cot, it was he who very gently lifted Baby Gabrielle up in his hands. The baby stretched and yawned, indignant almost at being disturbed, and for Louise, watching, the moment was somehow unbearably poignant. This was a situation she had found herself in several times before as it was often necessary for a baby to be baptised on the unit, but somehow this time it was different, and at the sight of her husband with this tiny baby cradled in his strong hands she found she had to fight a huge lump that had risen in her throat. Taking the shawl from the baby's grandmother, Matt placed the baby on it then gently passed the infant to her mother.

The words of the simple baptism ceremony were beautiful and incredibly moving as they all bore witness to Baby Gabrielle being welcomed into the family of God. Mike asked Julie to name the child then as he baptised her with the holy water and made the sign of the cross on her tiny forehead, his big, distinctive voice was softened now to fit the circumstances. 'Gabrielle Julie, I baptise you in the name of the Father and of the Son and of the Holy Spirit.'

It was only then that Louise dared a glance at Matt, only to find there were tears in his eyes. Finding the sight somehow unbearable, she was forced to look quickly away.

Afterwards they all made their way to the relatives' room where Sister Lane gave everyone a glass of sherry and several photographs were taken by Gabrielle's grandfather before the little girl was taken back onto the ward to be prepared for surgery.

As Matt and Louise signalled to each other and would have slipped quietly away, Julie and Russell came across to them. 'Thank you,' said Julie simply, looking from one to the other, 'thank you both.'

'It was our privilege,' said Matt, shaking hands with Russell.

'Somehow it's strengthened me for what we have to face next,' Julie said quietly.

'It was a beautiful ceremony,' Louise agreed.

'It made us realise we want to get married,' said Russell. 'We had thought about it before talking to Mike, and now, well, we know it's what we want, don't we, love?' He put his arm around Julie and looked down at her.

'Yes.' She nodded then had to brush away the tears that trickled down her cheeks. 'We thought we were quite happy just living together, that we didn't need a piece of paper to prove our love for each other, but somehow…all this…has made us think…'

In silence Louise and Matt left SCBU and began walking down the corridor to the main reception.

'I wonder,' said Louise, at last breaking the silence, 'if

things would have been different for us if we'd simply just lived together and not attempted to get married.'

'Who knows?' said Matt with a sigh. 'At the time it seemed the right thing to do but I suppose we would still have argued in time whether we were married or not.'

'Yes,' Louise agreed, 'I dare say we would.'

'There were good times as well, though, weren't there?' he said after a moment.

'Of course there were.' Somehow, in spite of herself, she found her gaze meeting his. This time the merriment was absent from those green eyes, replaced by an anxiousness tinged almost with sadness.

'We…we were good together once,' he said slowly, and a new light crept into his eyes, a light she remembered only too well.

'Yes, Matt, we were,' she said firmly, 'but—'

'Sometimes I can't believe it all went so wrong and I don't really understand why it did.'

'I think we may have let our careers get in the way.'

'Maybe…' He shrugged then suddenly his pager went off, shattering the silence and destroyed the intensity of the moment. With a muttered exclamation he took it from his pocket and switched it off. 'I have to go,' he said almost regretfully, as if he would far rather stay here in the corridor, talking to her and discussing why their relationship hadn't worked. 'Neil will be gunning for me.' He paused. 'I was wondering, Louise, about those things of mine at the house. Could I call round this evening for them?'

'No, Matt, not this evening,' she said. 'I'm going to Michelle's for a dress fitting.'

'I see. Well, how about tomorrow evening?'

'Yes, all right,' she heard herself say. 'Tomorrow will be fine.'

CHAPTER FOUR

IT WAS quite true what Matt had said, Louise thought as she made her way from the hospital to the staff car park. It had been good between them once—in fact, it had been very good. The sexual chemistry had been there from the very beginning when she had first found herself looking into those devastating green eyes of his, and it had simmered through the early days of their relationship until, at last, there had been an opportunity for them to be completely alone together.

It had finally come one evening when Michelle had been visiting a friend in London and Louise and Matt had just returned to the flat after visiting the cinema. Louise had been about to make coffee when Michelle had phoned to say she was staying overnight with her friend. They had both known what was going to happen from the moment Louise had put the phone down and had told Matt what Michelle had said.

'So we're alone at last.' Following her into the kitchen, he slid his arms around her as she stood at the sink, filling the kettle.

'It seems like it,' she replied, briefly leaning against him.

'I was getting quite desperate, wondering how I was ever going to get you to myself.' Slowly he began kissing the soft hollow between her neck and shoulder and she felt little shudders of delight course up and down her spine. 'Michelle and Andy are great,' he went on, 'but sometimes...I have to confess...I so wanted it to be just us...'

The coffee was forgotten, the kettle abandoned on the draining-board as she had turned and slipped naturally into his arms, giving herself up to the delight of being kissed by him.

From there, as their desire for one another grew to fever pitch, it seemed the most natural thing in the world to progress to Louise's bedroom where she soon discovered that making love with Matt was more exciting than anything she could have imagined. He was a skilled and tender lover, fully mindful of her needs before his own, rousing her to heights undreamed of and satisfying her in a way that left her helpless with delight.

When at last they slept he was right there in her dreams and when she awoke the next morning, she simply lay there beside him for a long time in the chill grey light of dawn, watching him sleep. When eventually he, too, woke up, she witnessed his initial surprise as for the briefest of moments she knew he wondered where he was then, on recalling, turned his head and found her beside him.

'Hi,' he said, his voice husky with sleep.

'Hi, yourself,' she replied. 'Did you sleep well?'

'Oh, yes,' he said. 'The best.' Without another word he reached out for her and they made love all over again, and if it was at all possible, this time it was even better.

And that, she thought as she secured her seat belt and switched on the ignition was how it had been between them before it had all gone so desperately wrong. Their times alone had been infinitely precious, if infrequent, because Matt himself had been living in hospital accommodation and the flat that Louise shared with Michelle had been very small and lacking in privacy.

As she drew out of the car park and onto the main road, still lost in her memories, she found herself recalling that one special weekend they had shared in Brighton. Matt had arranged it all, booking a hotel on the seafront where after a romantic candle-lit dinner for two they had strolled together along the promenade in the moonlight. Following a night of tender, shared love they had spent the following morning exploring the many fascinating shops in The Lanes and the afternoon walking on the beach in the fresh, bracing sea air.

And it had been there, as gulls had circled and wheeled above, their cries mingling with the sound of the waves as they'd broken on the shingle, that the question of marriage had first been broached.

They'd quickly discovered that neither felt they were ready for marriage and that both needed to concentrate on their careers, which were of paramount importance.

'That's not to say that I won't want to marry one day,' Matt said, holding her hand tightly as they backed away from a particularly large wave. 'But I have more training to go through yet which I can't do at Ellie's and, quite honestly, I can't see marriage fitting in.'

'Nor me,' she replied, and she could remember saying it, she thought now with a tight little smile as she drew up in front of the house. 'I have already set myself career goals,' she'd added, 'and reaching them certainly doesn't include marriage…or children.'

'Ah, children,' he'd said, slipping his arm around her and hugging her against him, 'well, that's something else. I certainly wouldn't be able to cope with children—not for some considerable time yet.'

'Me neither,' she'd agreed with a little shudder. 'Again, like you, I'm not saying that isn't something I would like one day—but, well, let's face it, there's plenty of time yet. I think it's so much more practical these days now that women are delaying starting their families—at least it gives them a chance to establish their careers and to enjoy life a bit before finally settling down.'

'My sentiments exactly,' he'd said, giving her another hug. 'I'm all for enjoying life a bit. Speaking of which, isn't it time we went back to the hotel?'

Now, as Louise thought about it, Matt's words seemed to echo hollowly in her ears until finally, with a little sigh, she climbed out of her car and entered the house.

'Hold still a minute, I just need to take this in a little bit. If you could raise your arms, that's it. There, all finished.'

Louise lowered her arms and, turning slightly, caught sight of herself in the oval bedroom mirror. The bodice of the dress she was wearing, decorated in dozens of tiny diamanté beads, hugged her figure while the skirt fell softly to the floor in gentle folds of cream satin. It looked good with her blonde hair and against her fresh complexion and she knew she would be happy wearing it on Michelle's big day. And, she thought ruefully, it was probably the closest she would ever come to wearing a conventional wedding dress herself. Her own had been vastly different from this wonderful creation.

'So how do I look?' At the sound of Michelle's voice from the doorway Louise turned sharply and the sight of her friend in her wedding dress almost took her breath away. The dress, in ivory satin, was a study in simplicity, straight and strapless with a long narrow train, its only adornment the beading that edged the bodice. Against Michelle's creamy skin and auburn hair the result was stunning.

'Oh, Michelle,' said Louise finding her voice at last, 'you look fantastic.'

'I think we just need a few little tucks here and there,'

muttered Mrs Nesbitt, the seamstress, as she knelt in front of Michelle, her mouth full of pins.

'Are Mollie and Jack coming in for a fitting?' asked Louise, referring to Michelle's little niece and Andy's nephew who were to be flower girl and pageboy.

'No.' Mrs Nesbitt shook her head and, speaking through the pins, added, 'they had their final fitting this afternoon after nursery school and I have to say they both look absolutely adorable.'

'Michelle…' A voice from the doorway made them turn to find Sue Burns, Michelle's mother, standing there with a mobile phone in her hand. As she caught sight of her daughter, however, she seemed for a moment to have been rendered speechless. 'Oh, darling,' she said at last, 'oh, you look beautiful… Just wait until your father sees you…'

'Thanks, Mum.' Michelle smiled and smoothed down the skirt of the dress, earning a tut and a rebuke from Mrs Nesbitt who begged her to keep still. 'Was there someone on that phone?' she asked when her mother simply continued to stare at her.

'Phone?' Sue Burns stared blankly at her daughter then looked down at the phone in her hand. 'Oh, yes,' she said at last. 'It's for you—Andy.' Crossing the room, she handed the phone to her daughter then turned and looked at Louise. 'Oh, Louise, you look lovely as well,' she said. 'I'm so glad you and Michelle decided on the cream—it really suits you.'

Vaguely, as she chatted to Sue, Louise was aware of Michelle speaking on the phone to Andy, and when at last Michelle switched off the mobile she could tell from her friend's expression there was something wrong.

'Michelle?' she said anxiously. 'What is it?'

'It's Andy's brother, Paul,' said Michelle slowly.

'What about him?' asked Sue.

'He's had an accident,' said Michelle, 'a car accident.'

'Oh, my God!' said Louise. 'Is he all right?'

'He has a broken femur and a back injury. He's in hospital in Plymouth so there's no way he's going to make the wedding.'

'But he's best man…' There was just a hint of hysteria in Sue's voice.

'Presumably a substitute best man can be found even at this late stage,' said Mrs Nesbitt as she struggled to her feet. She spoke with the world-weary tone of someone who has heard every possible pre-wedding source of panic.

'Michelle…?' There was a wild look in Sue's eye now.

'Yes.' Michelle nodded and from the expression on her face as she looked at her, Louise knew what she was going to say even before she said it. 'Andy has asked Matt,' she said, 'and Matt's agreed.'

'I'm sorry, Louise,' said Michelle later after Mrs Nesbitt had gone and she and Louise were alone, enjoying a glass of wine together, 'this is going to be difficult for you, isn't it?'

'Well, it might not be exactly easy,' said Louise with a little shrug, 'but I dare say I'll survive. After all, I'd got used to the idea that Matt was coming to the wedding. I guess being best man won't mean too much more.'

'No,' Michelle agreed, 'although the best man and the chief bridesmaid do sort of get lumped together, if you know what I mean—photographs and first dance and all that.'

'Do you mind? Attendant, please,' protested Louise. 'I'm hardly bridesmaid material at my age. And in any case, technically I'm married.'

'Yes, well, whatever.' Michelle shrugged and took a large mouthful of her wine. 'My God,' she said, 'this wedding business really is stressful.'

'Don't worry, we won't have a slanging match at the altar or anything like that,' said Louise with a chuckle then, as an afterthought, added, 'Talking of stress, I thought your mum was going to have a nervous breakdown on the spot just now.'

'Mmm, me too,' agreed Michelle. 'She does worry so—about everything. I don't know how many times she's checked all the arrangements. She's constantly on the phone to the caterers and the florist—they must be sick of her by now.'

'She just wants it all to be perfect for you,' said Louise.

'Yes, I know.' Michelle sighed. 'And really I'm grateful to her and to Dad—honestly, it must all be costing them a fortune, but they insisted this was the way they wanted it.' She paused. 'But do you know, Lou, I sometimes wonder whether you didn't have the right idea, the way you did things, with absolutely no fuss.'

'I don't know.' Louise shook her head. 'My parents weren't too happy about it and that's putting it mildly.... And at the end of the day it didn't work out, did it?'

'No,' agreed Michelle with a little sigh, 'I guess it didn't.'

'Have we heard how Gabrielle is?' asked Nicky. It was the following morning and Louise had just begun her shift.

'Yes, apparently she came through the operation very well,' Louise replied. 'Both Mr Green and Mr Richardson are pleased with her. Her condition is still critical, of course, and she'll be in Intensive Care for the next few days, but hopefully, after that, she'll be able to return to us.'

'Are Julie and Russell with her?'

'Yes, they stayed the night.' Louise looked up as ward clerk Gina unlocked the unit doors and admitted a woman called Pauline Cleaver, the first of the day's visitors. Pauline's daughter Beth had been born prematurely three weeks previously, weighing less than two and a half pounds, and she had been cared for on the unit ever since. Pauline had two older children at home to care for, which meant that the time she spent with Beth was probably not as much as she would have liked.

'Good morning, Sister Keating.' Pauline looked strained and tired. 'Is she all right today?' It was the same question she asked every morning on her arrival, a question heavy with dread and anxiety.

'She's fine, Pauline,' Louise hastened to reassure her, knowing only too well the stress that was suffered by the parents of the tiny babies who were born before their time. 'Maybe you would like to wash and dress her this morning?'

'Yes, I would.' A smile touched Pauline's mouth. 'I'll go and get scrubbed up.' It was a strict rule that anyone entering the unit washed their hands, and if they were going to be handling a baby they were required to scrub up with iodine. Louise and Nicky watched as Pauline took herself off to the sluice then Louise began sorting through the pile of patient folders on her desk.

'Oliver doesn't seem so alert this morning,' said Nicky. 'I noticed when I was replacing his nasogastric tube—he seems rather lethargic.'

'I'll ask Dr Forrester to have a look at him,' said Louise, making a note on her pad.

'I think you'll need to have a chat with his mum, Tracey, as well,' said Nicky. 'She was very agitated yesterday. She'll be even more so now if there's anything wrong.'

'Is she here yet?' Louise looked round.

'No, Elaine has gone to get her.'

'Good.' Louise nodded. 'Once Dr Forrester has checked

Oliver, and if there isn't too much wrong, I suggest we start involving Tracey with his care as soon as we can.'

They continued discussing the care of the other babies on the ward until Matt arrived, together with Sandie Rawlings. After scrubbing up, the two doctors joined Louise and Nicky for a ward round.

'Mr Richardson is in a meeting,' said Matt cheerfully, 'so I'm afraid you have to put up with us this morning.'

'I'm sure we'll survive, Dr Forrester,' said Louise calmly, meeting his half-amused gaze before leading the way onto the ward.

By this time Tracey had arrived from Maternity and was sitting alongside Oliver's incubator. She looked a little better that morning, Louise noticed, as, no doubt, she was now recovering more fully from her Caesarean section.

'Ah, yes,' said Matt, reaching into the incubator and touching Oliver's forehead, 'this is our little business tycoon, isn't it? Now, let's have a look.' Taking the chart that Louise handed to him, he carefully studied the details of Oliver's care plan, together with the baby's reactions to the treatment and medication he was receiving.

'Hmm,' he said at last, passing the reports back to Louise, 'he's certainly less jaundiced than he was, although I would like to keep the phototherapy treatment up for a while yet.' He paused, looking down at Oliver. 'Now, has he started feeding?'

'Yes.' Louise nodded. 'Tracey's been expressing her milk and he's being fed through his nasogastric tube.'

'That's good.' Gently Matt examined Baby Oliver, warming his stethoscope before applying it to the tiny chest and abdomen, all the time watched anxiously by Tracey. After completing his examination, he lifted Oliver out of the incubator and held him for a while, cradling his head in one hand and supporting his body in the other. 'I may have to change the dose and strength of his medication,' he said at last.

'Why?' demanded Tracey. 'What's wrong with him?'

'I don't think there's any cause for alarm at all,' said Matt calmly. 'I think he may probably have a slight infection, possibly in his urine, but we won't take any chances and we'll do some tests just to make sure.'

'What sort of tests?' There was a wild look in Tracey's eyes now.

'Just blood tests and urine tests to start with,' explained Louise gently.

'What do you mean, to start with?' Tracey was clearly far from happy. 'What else will you have to do?'

'Hopefully, nothing,' replied Matt reassuringly. 'The tests should tell us all we need to know so that if necessary we can arrange appropriate medication.'

'Will Joe be coming in today?' asked Louise a few moments later as Matt and Sandie, after further words of reassurance, moved on to the next baby.

'Not until later,' said Tracey miserably. 'He's had to go back to work. I think I might phone him, though.'

'Don't alarm him,' said Louise. 'I'm sure there isn't any need to worry.' Leaving Nicky to arrange Oliver's tests, Louise caught up with Matt and Sandie who by this time were checking on Liam Kerrigan's progress.

'He really is doing very well,' said Matt, as he looked down at the baby who was awake and appeared to be staring up intently at the circle of faces around his cot. 'He's feeding well and gaining weight, there are no breathing problems and the jaundice I see he suffered at birth has cleared up. I think very soon we may be looking at him going home.' He looked at Louise. 'Is his mum coming in today?'

'Oh, yes,' Louise replied, 'I'm sure she will be. She comes in every day. She'll be delighted.'

'Well, I'll have a word with Mr Richardson but I think you could start to prepare her.'

'If he clears it, we'll arrange for Lisa to come and stay for a couple of days so that she can get used to caring for him before he goes home,' said Louise.

'Excellent, Sister,' said Matt, meeting her eye. 'Now, who do we have next?'

'Beth, Dr Forrester,' Louise replied. 'Baby Beth Cleaver.'

At the end of the ward round, while Sandie slipped back to talk to Nicky and Tracey about Oliver, Matt followed Louise into her office.

'Louise,' he said, glancing over his shoulder to make sure they couldn't be overheard, 'did you go to Michelle's last night?'

'I did.' She nodded coolly.

'Did she say anything about…about the wedding?' There was an air of embarrassment about him and Louise could guess what was coming.

'Considering I was there for a dress fitting,' she said, 'we talked of little else.'

'Well, yes, quite, but—'

'If you mean did she tell me that you are to be best man then, yes, she did.'

'Actually, I didn't know quite what to say,' said Matt, looking relieved that Louise knew. 'It put me in a bit of a spot when Andy asked me. After all, he's a good mate and his brother's accident has put him in a fix what with the wedding being so close and all that.'

'Why should it have put you in a spot?' asked Louise.

'Well, I thought with you being a bridesmaid and all that—'

'Attendant,' she interrupted.

'Sorry?' He frowned.

'I'm Michelle's attendant. You said bridesmaid and I'm hardly that.'

'Oh, really? Well, no, I suppose not.' He looked embarrassed again almost as if he wished he hadn't mentioned it. 'It's just that I've wondered since whether you might be upset about it.'

'Upset?' Louise raised her eyebrows, aware that her heart had started to beat rather fast and afraid that Matt might in some way be able to detect that and thereby know that, yes, it had upset her, knowing he was to be best man. She couldn't say why that should be exactly, she just knew it did. Maybe it was something to do with the fact that they would be standing there right behind Michelle and Andy as they exchanged their vows at the altar, or maybe it was, as Michelle had implied, that they might be the butt of people's jokes, those who knew their situation and even those who didn't. 'Why should I be upset?' she asked.

'I don't know.' He shrugged, looking even more uncomfortable. 'I just thought you might.'

'No.' She shook her head. 'The way I see it is that Michelle is my friend and she has asked me to perform a task for her. Andy is your friend and he has asked the same of you...'

'Yes, I know. It's just that our circumstances being what they are...I thought perhaps that you might feel uncomfortable or that other people might...'

'Might what?' Louise raised her eyebrows again. 'Read more into it than they should?'

'Well, yes, something like that, I suppose...' he muttered miserably.

'I'm sure we needn't worry about that and, besides, even if they did, they'll soon learn otherwise, won't they?'

'Yes, absolutely.' Matt nodded and seemed to pull himself together. As he moved to the door he paused and with one hand on the handle looked back. 'Is it still all right for me to come round this evening?'

'Er, yes, of course.' She tried to sound vague, sorting through papers on her desk as if the whole thing was of little importance when in reality the very thought of Matt coming to the house still filled her with apprehension.

'You don't sound very sure,' he said.

'What?' She looked up sharply to find him still standing there, looking at her.

'About me coming to the house.'

'Oh, no, of course I am. That's all right, Matt. I'll see you later.'

'About six o'clock?'

'Yes, six o'clock will be fine.'

He went then, leaving Louise struggling to dismiss from her mind the disturbing elements of her private life and to pick up the threads of the running of her busy unit.

She barely had a chance to draw breath before Nicky tapped on the door to inform her that Lisa had just arrived.

'Ask her to come in, would you, Nicky?' said Louise.

Lisa looked tired and anxious when Nicky showed her into the office a few minutes later. 'Is there anything wrong, Sister Keating?' she asked, sitting down on the chair that Louise indicated. 'Liam is all right, isn't he? Yesterday he seemed fine…' She trailed off as Louise lifted her hand and hastened to reassure her.

'Lisa, please, Liam is fine. There's nothing to worry about.' Louise knew from experience how the slightest thing could set a mother thinking there was something wrong, from a simple request for a chat in her office to an unexpected phone call, because so often in the past there *had* been something wrong as—and especially in Liam's case—these tiny premature babies fought for their lives. Very often the path wasn't a smooth one and was fraught with dangers and obstacles, all of which had to be overcome with the skill and dedication of the staff and the patience and courage of the parents.

'You really mean that?' said Lisa as she looped her hair back behind her ears. 'There isn't another setback, is there?'

'No, not at all. In fact, just the opposite.' Louise smiled. 'Dr Forrester has just been in to see Liam and he says that he doesn't see any reason why we shouldn't be talking about him going home soon.'

'Oh!' Lisa's hand flew to her mouth and tears of joy filled her eyes. 'Oh, do you really mean that?'

'Of course. He's a good weight now—just a few ounces over five pounds—and he's feeding well. I know there was a little blip with his feeding the other day but we sorted that out and he's fine now.'

'I can't believe it.' Lisa dashed away the tears that had spilled over and were running down her cheeks. 'It's been such a long time and he had such problems with his breathing. There were times when I thought…when I feared…'

'I know, Lisa.' Louise reached out and gently touched Lisa's shoulder. 'But that's all behind you, it's in the past. All you and Shawn have to do now is to look forward to taking Liam home and caring for him yourselves.'

'I shall be afraid at first,' admitted Lisa shakily. 'He's still so small. I shall be so worried that something will go wrong…that I might be doing things wrong.'

'That's what I wanted to talk to you about,' said Louise. 'What I suggest is that before Liam is discharged you come and stay in the relatives' unit. We'll move Liam in there with you and you can take charge of his care yourself for a couple of days, just to get you into the routine. Shawn can join you, of course, whenever he can. When you do take Liam home you'll have backup from the community team and your health visitor. Now…' Louise stood up and indicated the phone on her desk '…why don't I leave you to phone Shawn and tell him the good news?'

'Oh, thank you, Sister,' said Lisa. 'Thank you so much for all you've done.'

'It's what we're here for,' said Louise gently.

As she left the room she heard Lisa say, 'Shawn? Oh, Shawn, it's me—guess what! You'll never believe this but…'

With a smile Louise slipped out of the room and quietly closed the door behind her.

CHAPTER FIVE

THE Eleanor James Memorial Hospital had been built in a delightful sylvan setting in the mid-1970s and named after the wife of its main benefactor who at that time had been Franchester's mayor. The building itself was constructed of yellow brick underneath a coral-tiled roof, giving it a vaguely Mediterranean feel, while the interior was modern and well equipped. Louise counted herself as fortunate to work there, never for one moment taking the setting or surroundings for granted.

She reversed out of her parking space onto the main driveway at the end of her shift, noting as she did so the quiet splendour of the two huge macrocarpa trees on the lawn, the mass of narcissus and jonquils that seemed to float above mossy grass banks and the majestic avenue of beeches that lined the drive all the way to the main road.

She drove down into the town where on a sudden impulse she parked at the supermarket and found herself buying a French loaf, a bottle of red Australian wine, some Camembert cheese and a bunch of grapes, all of which were Matt's favourites—which was quite ridiculous under the circumstances, she told herself angrily as she got back into the car. After all, he was only coming to pick up some of his belongings, for heaven's sake—it wasn't exactly going to be a social call.

On the other hand, she reasoned, hadn't they called a sort of truce until after the wedding, delaying the moment when they would have to end the farce that their own marriage had become? And besides, she would have to offer him something and she knew she had very little in the house so surely it made sense to buy something she knew he liked?

Having allowed her reasoning to square her conscience, she drove home, parked outside the house and hurried inside. After changing into jeans and a sweatshirt, she found she had over an hour to spare before Matt was due to arrive. To pass the time she wandered outside into the garden at the rear of the house. Secluded and enclosed by walls of pink brick, Louise loved her garden—from the borders alight with polyanthus and pansies at this time of year to the elegant sweep of heathers and dwarf conifers taking up one entire side and the decking area beneath a wooden pergola that throughout the year would have clematis tumbling from its rafters, then wisteria, and finally, as summer came into its own, glorious cream roses. The garden had been one of the deciding factors when she and Matt had bought the house, and already Louise knew it would break her heart to leave it.

She hadn't intended doing any gardening that day but once out there in the tranquil peace of the spring evening it became irresistible and she found herself automatically tidying up, which led to a spot of weeding, which in turn led to sorting through the pots and containers that would eventually house her early summer bedding plants. She tried not to think about the fact that she might no longer be in the house to see those same bedding plants bloom. Maybe, she thought hopefully, the house wouldn't sell for ages, well, not until the end of summer anyway...

Gardening relaxed her, it always did, especially after a demanding day on the unit. Today was no exception and gradually, in spite of the fact that she had been apprehensive all day about Matt coming to the house and to a certain extent still was, as she worked with the soft rich soil, she felt her tension slip away.

She became so absorbed in what she was doing that when the doorbell finally sounded in the house behind her she jumped and glanced frantically at her watch, realising that it was the time they had agreed for Matt to come. She hadn't meant to stay in the garden for so long, she had meant to give herself time to go back into the house and wash her hands, tidy her hair, maybe even to put on a touch of lipstick—but there was no time for that now, and as she hurried through the house the doorbell sounded for a second time.

She pulled open the door and found Matt standing on the step looking down the road then raising his hand to someone out of sight before turning to look at her.

'I thought perhaps you were out,' he said.

'No...' She half leaned forward, curious as to who he was waving to.

'That was Angelo,' Matt explained. 'He's gone now...'

No doubt to tell Maria he's seen Matt coming into the house, thought Louise as she stepped aside for Matt to enter the narrow hallway. 'I was in the garden,' she said, as much for something to say than by way of an explanation.

'So how is the garden?' he asked.

'Come and see for yourself.' She closed the front door and led the way through the house to the rear then outside, where Matt stood beside her on the decking looking around him at the garden he had once tended with almost as much enthusiasm as she had.

'It's looking good,' he said at last, and Louise felt a sudden surge of pride that she had managed to keep the garden well tended in his absence. Not that it really made any difference now, of course. After all, it wasn't as if he

was taking the garden over, unless, of course, he bought
her out as he had suggested he might. She dismissed the
thought as soon as it re-entered her mind. She hadn't liked
it when he had first spoken of it, she liked it even less
when she thought of it in conjunction with her beloved
garden. 'How were the roses last summer?' He looked
above him at the pergola where the clematis was just coming into leaf.

'Wonderful,' she said. 'It was so mild and they seemed
to go on and on—there was even one in bloom a couple
of weeks before Christmas.'

'I thought about them,' he said ruefully, 'in my little
concrete jungle.'

'Didn't you have any garden?' she asked, suddenly realising she knew nothing of what Matt's life had been like
in Scotland.

'There were flower-beds around the hospital entrance,'
he said, 'but the accommodation block I was in was pretty
bleak.'

'Did you stay there all the time?' she asked as they
turned and made their way back into the house.

'Where else would I go?'

'I don't know—I just wondered.'

'I made a conscious effort not to come back here, if
that's what you mean,' he said carefully.

'I didn't mean—' Louise began, but he silenced her,
stretching out his hand and unexpectedly touching her
face. She froze at the touch of his fingers on her cheek.
'What...?' she said.

'You've got soil on your face,' he said calmly. 'Keep
still—there, that's better, it's gone. Now, where were we?
Oh, yes, I was saying about not coming back here during
the last year. Like I say, it was deliberate on my part. We

had agreed to separate and I thought after a year apart we would pretty well know what we wanted to do.'

'Well, yes, I suppose so.' Moving away from him, Louise rubbed her cheek where she could still feel the touch of his fingers. 'So you stayed there in Scotland all the time?'

'More or less. I did get out and see a bit of the countryside during my time off, although I have to say most of that was spent studying. I did get down to see my sister Elizabeth for one weekend.'

'What about Christmas?' Suddenly she was curious. She herself had spent Christmas with her parents. 'What did you do then?'

'Oh, I got invited to a friend's for that,' he said casually.

She wanted to ask about his friends, these unknown people who had taken her husband in at Christmas, no doubt because they'd felt sorry for him, being in a strange town on his own over the festive season, but somehow she didn't quite dare. Instead, she said, 'I guess we'd better go and sort out your things.'

'Yes, all right.' He nodded then, as she led the way, followed her from the kitchen into the dining room.

'I wasn't sure what you wanted to take now,' she said. 'There are these.' She paused, looking down at the table on which she had placed a neat pile of CDs and a few videos. 'There are also all your books, your camera, some clothes and some folders of work. And we will, of course, need to divide other things—items we bought together...' She trailed off as she realised he wasn't listening, that he had picked up some of the CDs and was looking through them. She couldn't see the expression on his face.

'Don't you want this one?' he asked at last, turning one of the cases so she could see the title. It was an album that contained a song they had once considered their own. As she struggled to find something to say, he shrugged. 'Maybe not,' he said. 'It's not exactly appropriate now, is it?'

'You bought it,' she said quietly. 'I thought you might want it.'

With another shrug Matt replaced the album then looked up. 'Did you say something about some clothes?'

'Yes, they're upstairs in the wardrobe. You can go up,' she added when he appeared to hesitate.

'OK,' he muttered. He left the room, leaving Louise standing there staring at the pile of albums on the table and wondering why all this seemed so painful when it was quite obviously what both of them wanted. She remembered exactly when Matt had bought that album. It had been after that wonderful weekend in Brighton when they had heard it being played all the time—on the car radio, snatches of it in shops or in restaurants…

A shout from upstairs jolted her out of her reverie. 'Louise, which wardrobe did you mean?'

She walked out of the dining room into the hall and looked up the stairs. Matt stood on the landing, peering over the banisters. 'The big wardrobe in…the main bedroom,' she said. She had almost said 'in our bedroom', only just stopping herself in time.

'Oh,' said Matt, and she couldn't help but hear the surprise in his voice. 'I thought you meant the one in the spare room.' He turned and went into the main bedroom, and with a little sigh Louise slowly climbed the stairs. When she reached the landing she had to take a deep breath, bracing herself to go into the room that she and Matt had once shared.

By the time she entered the room Matt had taken his leather coat, suit and several other items from the wardrobe. He looked up as she entered the room. 'I thought

you would have chucked all my things into the other room
by now,' he said, 'but that wardrobe was full of your
clothes…' He glanced around the room and Louise noticed
his puzzled look.

'I've been using that room,' she said at last, 'since you
left…'

'Oh,' he said. 'I see.' For a moment he looked almost
hurt, as if he thought she couldn't even bear to be reminded of how they had once been.

'You don't have to take all that now,' she said quickly,
more to change the subject than anything, 'not if you don't
have room at the moment. Besides, if you plan on buying
me out they may as well stay here anyway—not much
point in moving them really.' She gave a sort of hopeless
little shrug.

'I've thought about that,' said Matt, holding up his suit
to the light and inspecting it.

'And…?' she said, finding she was holding her breath
as she waited for his reply.

'I don't really think it's such a good idea after all.'

'Ah,' she said, letting her breath go. 'Really?' she
added, hoping she sounded casual.

'No.' He shook his head. Then, looking up from the suit,
he said, 'I think we both perhaps need to make a fresh
start. Don't you?' he added.

'Oh, yes,' she agreed. 'Yes, absolutely.' Louise was relieved he wasn't going to buy her out, relieved he wasn't
going to be living here in this house without her, tending
the garden, being there, maybe in time with someone
else… But at the same time, perversely, hearing him talk
of fresh starts suddenly and unexpectedly depressed her.

'I was thinking I would need this suit for the wedding,'
he said after a moment, seemingly oblivious to her turmoil,
'and I guess it would have been OK if I was just going to

be a guest, but Andy tells me it's to be morning dress so I need to get myself down to the outfitter's tomorrow to get measured up for a hire suit.'

'You could leave your coat here for the time being,' Louise suggested. 'I doubt you'll be needing that, with the summer coming.'

'Good idea. I'll do that, if it's all right with you.'

'Yes, of course.' Suddenly the incongruity of the situation hit her—that she and Matt, this man who had once meant the world to her, should be standing there in the room that had been theirs, at the foot of the bed they had once shared, as they divided their possessions. How in the world had they come to this?

Suddenly, as she battled with her thoughts and emotions Louise became intensely aware of Matt beside her. She only had to reach out her hand and she could touch him. Even by looking at him, she could imagine the feel of the fabric of his sweater, the slight roughness of his jaw, the pressure of his arms around her. And all that only one step away, as was the sweetness of his lips against hers, the sensation of him running his fingers through her hair in just the way he used to. And from there it would be but a hair's breadth to sinking down onto the softness of the bed that had once been theirs, to throw caution to the winds, to give themselves up completely to the delight of the love they had once shared…

'Now…' Matt looked round the bedroom again and the moment was lost. 'Where were those folders you mentioned?'

'On top of the wardrobe,' she replied shakily.

'Well, I'll just get those—then I suppose I'd better be going.'

'Do you have to rush away?' she asked as he stood on a chair and retrieved the pile of folders.

'No, not really.'

'You're welcome to stay for a snack.'

'I've probably taken up enough of your time as it is.'

'No, it's OK,' she said lightly. 'I was going to have something to eat anyway. Like I say, you're welcome to join me.'

'Oh, well,' he replied, 'in that case, if you're sure, yes, I'd love to. Thanks.'

He followed Louise downstairs and while she set out the simple meal—the bread and cheese and the grapes—and poured a couple of glasses of wine, he studied the contents of his folders.

'These could be useful,' he said at last, looking up. 'In fact, I could have done with some of this stuff when I was in Scotland.'

'You should have let me know,' Louise replied. 'I could have sent it on to you.'

'To be honest, I'd forgotten a lot of it was there. Still, never mind, I can probably put some of it to use now—nothing is ever wasted in terms of studying, not in my experience anyway. I say...' He paused and looked at the table. 'You shouldn't have gone to all that trouble—you said a snack.'

'It's no trouble, Matt, it's only bread and cheese.'

'Which just happens to be Camembert. And Australian wine,' he added, leaning forward to take a look at the label.

'Yes, well.' She shrugged. 'I had to go to the super-market on the way home so I just picked up a few things.' Suddenly she felt uncomfortable, afraid that he should think she had gone to inordinate lengths to please him. 'So, how is your training going?' she asked in an attempt to change the subject as they sat down at the table.

'Very well, actually.' He nodded. 'Scotland was amazing and I have to say it's very, very good to be on Neil

Richardson's team—and Ellie's special care baby unit is, well, simply the best.'

'But of course,' said Louise, then, raising her glass, said, 'Shall we drink to that?'

'Absolutely,' he replied. Raising his own glass, he said, 'The unit.'

'The unit,' echoed Louise.

They were silent for a moment, each reflecting, and then Matt spoke. 'I take it you are happy there?'

'Oh, yes.' She nodded. 'Very happy.'

'Well, it was what you always wanted, wasn't it?' He spoke lightly, without apparently any trace of irony, but Louise found herself casting him a searching glance. His expression, however, was as unambiguous as his tone.

'Yes,' she agreed, after she had satisfied herself that his question wasn't loaded, 'it was exactly what I wanted. And now,' she couldn't resist adding, 'you also are getting to where you always wanted to be.'

'True,' he replied. Whilst apparently studying the contents of his glass he said casually, 'Are you all right now, Louise? You know what I mean, after—'

'Yes, I'm fine,' she said quickly, interrupting him before he could go any further.

'Good.' He paused. 'It's just that I…I have wondered and…'

'No, Matt,' she said, 'let's not talk about it. I didn't ask you here for that.'

'I know you didn't,' he said quietly, 'but maybe we should talk about it.'

'What's the point? It's over, in the past, and there's absolutely nothing we can do about it.'

'Like our marriage, you mean?' Raising his eyes from his wineglass, he allowed his gaze to meet hers.

'Yes,' she said uncertainly. 'Yes,' she repeated with a little more conviction, 'just like that—I suppose.'

Matt was silent for a moment, his gaze still steadily meeting hers until in the end she was forced to look away. 'I thought,' she said briskly as she leaned forward and cut herself a wedge of Camembert, 'we'd agreed not to discuss the state of our marriage until after Michelle's and Andy's wedding.'

'OK.' He shrugged. 'As you wish.' He paused then, popping a grape into his mouth, said, 'So what do you want to talk about?'

'How about you tell me about these friends that you spent Christmas with?' She hadn't meant to say that but ended up saying the first thing that came into her head.

'Not a lot to tell really.' He took a mouthful of wine.

'Were they colleagues?'

'Sort of.' He paused then, as if making up his mind, said, 'Serena was a radiologist on the unit I was working on.'

'Serena?' Louise stared at him, momentarily shocked that the friend he'd mentioned should have been a woman—which was ridiculous really because there was no earthly reason why it shouldn't have been. It was just that she had assumed he had been talking about a male colleague, a fellow SHO.

'Yes, Serena Stewart. I met her in the canteen one lunchtime,' Matt went on—quite casually, Louise thought, just as if he were discussing the weather. 'We got talking and I suppose she felt sorry for me, being on my own at Christmas. Her family lives just outside Aviemore.... Her father and brothers are in forestry.'

'Did she know you were married?' asked Louise.

'She knew I was separated,' replied Matt carefully.

She fell silent. Suddenly the French bread tasted like

sawdust. She pushed her plate away and poured more wine into Matt's glass then topped up her own. She should have guessed that he might have been seeing someone else during his time in Scotland, but it had never crossed her mind that it might have been the case—not once. She had been under the impression that it had been the same for Matt as it had for her—all work, very little social life and that there would be no romantic involvements, at least not until they had finally resolved their own situation. Which, really, now she came to think of it, had been nothing if not naïve. Matt was an incredibly attractive man, a virile, red-blooded man with normal healthy appetites. It was probably inconceivable that he should have remained alone and celibate for a whole year and, as he had just taken the trouble to point out, they *were* separated after all, which he had probably seen as giving him the leeway to do as he pleased. How foolish of her not to have suspected…

And what about now that she did know? Did it make any difference? she asked herself as she sat there, sipping her wine and watching Matt tuck heartily into the remainder of the bread and cheese.

Of course it didn't. Why should it? Why, here they were on the very brink of divorce, with only their friends' forthcoming wedding acting as an obstacle. And when that was over, the solicitors would swing into action, the house would be sold and they would be free to pick up the pieces and carry on with the rest of their lives. So why should it matter to her that her husband—because when all was said and done that was what he still was, separated or not— had become friendly with a Scottish radiologist called Serena?

'So what have you been doing with yourself for the past year?' he said at last, breaking into her thoughts and looking up from his food.

'Mainly work,' she replied with a little shrug. 'And after work, what with the house and the garden, there seems to have been little time for much else.' She was aware that an edge had crept into her voice.

'Surely you had some social life?' He frowned.

'A little,' she agreed. 'I've been to the social club with the girls a few times or to Angelo's for the occasional meal. I went to the theatre in Chichester just before Christmas,' she went on. Warming to her theme, she added, 'Oh, yes, and once, believe it or not, I went clubbing.'

'Clubbing?' He raised his eyebrows. 'Doesn't sound like you.'

'No, it doesn't, does it?' She gave a short laugh. 'A couple of the doctors on Orthopaedics got up a party. It...it was quite an experience.'

'But not your cup of tea.'

'Oh, I don't know. I wouldn't say that exactly.'

'But you never liked clubbing.' He looked surprised.

'I wouldn't go so far as to say I never liked it,' she protested mildly.

'Well, you certainly always gave that impression.'

'I'll have you know that in my youth, in the days of my training—before you came on the scene—Michelle and I could bop the night away with the best of them.'

'So are you saying you actually enjoyed it?' Matt still sounded faintly incredulous and Louise decided, on the spur of the moment, to embellish the truth a little. She wasn't entirely sure why, but she had the feeling it might have something to do with a certain radiologist. The last thing she wanted was for Matt to think that she had been sitting here at home, moping, while he had been living it up in Aviemore. 'Actually, yes, I did,' she said. 'It was great fun. I drank far too much and was on the dance floor nearly all night. Those guys from Ortho are great fun…'

'Did Andy go?' asked Matt curiously.

'No.' Louise shook her head. 'Neither did Michelle. I went with Nicky Edmunds, she's one of the staff nurses on my unit…'

'Yes,' said Matt, and Louise thought he sounded slightly irritated, 'I know who Nicky is.'

After that there was no more talk of what they had done in their year of separation, and when they had finished eating Louise made coffee, which she carried to the sitting room on a tray. The conversation stayed on safe topics, general things like the NHS and the fact that Maria Fabiano's father had recently died in Milan—anything rather than those personal issues which could be painful and which they had already agreed should be put on ice for the time being.

When they had finished their coffee Matt stood up. 'I must be going,' he said, picking up those of his belongings that he had decided to take. 'Thanks for the meal, Louise.'

'It was nothing.' She made a quick, dismissive gesture then followed him to the door. She tugged it open and they stood for an awkward moment on the step, with neither of them knowing, it seemed, quite what else to say or how to take their leave of each other. In the end, Matt lightly touched her cheek, the gesture friendly yet at the same time disturbingly intimate—so much so that she was glad when he moved away.

'See you tomorrow,' he said, and there was that same sad, rueful smile on his face that she had seen there several times since his return.

'Yes.' She nodded. 'See you tomorrow.' She stood for a moment, watching him walk away, but when she turned and closed the door it was to find that her heart was as heavy as lead.

CHAPTER SIX

'SHE'S going to die, isn't she?' The girl, who couldn't have been more than sixteen herself, seemed unable to look at the tiny figure of her baby daughter lying in an incubator.

'Not if we can help it,' replied Louise firmly. Even as they watched, Matt and Sandie arrived to examine the baby and decide on its treatment. Knowing that this would involve blood tests and other procedures which the young mother might find distressing, Louise turned to her. 'Why don't we go to my office for a while and leave the doctors to help Skye—that is the name you've chosen for her, isn't it?' she added, as with no further persuasion Rosie Bradley followed her to her office.

'This is my fault,' the girl said, even before Louise had closed the door behind them.

'Coffee?' asked Louise. 'I'm just going to make some.'

'Don't drink coffee.' The girl shook her head.

'What makes you think it's your fault?' Louise busied herself with the coffee-machine anyway.

'It's my punishment,' said Rosie. 'I was going to have an abortion.'

'But you didn't, did you?' Louise turned to look at the girl, taking in the long flowing fair hair—some thin sections of which were braided and bound with silver bands— the gold hoops in her ears and the tiny jewelled stud that pierced her nose. She'd only given birth the previous day and was still wearing a hospital gown and green striped dressing-gown, which suggested she'd not brought any of her own nightclothes to the hospital.

She shook her head in reply to Louise's question. 'I thought I might have it…her adopted,' she said.

'But why? Don't you want to keep her?' Louise sat down while she waited for the coffee.

'I can't.' Rosie shook her head and Louise noticed her mouth was set in a firm, sullen line. 'We're on the road…it's not possible.'

'So you're travellers?' Louise found she wasn't in the least surprised and could well imagine Rosie dressed in flowing, ethnic-style clothes.

'Yes, we're on the move most of the time…'

'But surely plenty of travellers have their children with them,' said Louise with a frown.

'But they said when she was born that she'll have to stay in here until she's reached her proper weight.'

'Yes, that's absolutely true.' Louise nodded then as the delicious aroma of fresh coffee filled the room she stood up and crossed to the machine. 'But afterwards when she's strong enough…'

'No, you don't understand.' Rosie shook her head and Louise caught the gleam of tears in her eyes.

'Are you sure you won't have that coffee?' she asked as she began pouring it into a mug.

'All right, then.' Rosie nodded. 'I only usually drink herbal tea—but that smells good. It reminds me…it reminds me of home.'

'So where is home, Rosie?' asked Louise as she poured another mug.

'Reading—well, that's where my parents live. I haven't lived there since…since…well, for a long time.'

'Do your parents know about the baby, Rosie?' asked Louise as she added milk to the two mugs of coffee then watched as Rosie added brown sugar to hers.

'No.' She shook her head then picked up the mug and

curled her thin hands around it. 'I haven't spoken to them for ages, ever since…I left home…'

'So they don't even know where you are, that you're safe, let alone that they have a grandchild?'

'No.' Rosie shook her head. 'I don't want them to know either,' she added—almost fiercely, Louise thought as she found herself wondering about Rosie's story.

'What do you think they would do if they knew?' she asked gently.

'They'd want me to go back…'

'Would that be so terrible—now that you have Skye, I mean?'

'Yes, it would.' Defiantly Rosie tilted her chin. 'You don't know what they're like. They drive me mad, always going on about what I wear and what time I come home. I'm not going back. Anyway the group's moving on soon—to Glastonbury. I've got to go with them,' she added, the determined note in her voice suddenly giving way to desperation.

'What about Skye's father, Rosie?' asked Louise casually.

'What *about* him?' said Rosie, immediately on the defensive.

'Well, is he supportive? Will he help you with Skye?'

'I s'ppose so,' she muttered. 'He wasn't happy when he knew I was pregnant…'

'Was that why you considered a termination?'

'Sort of. Anyway, that's why I think it would be better if she was adopted.'

'But at the moment, Rosie, Skye needs you,' said Louise gently. 'She needs her mum here beside her as she grows stronger and ready to face the world.'

'Yeah, I guess.' Rosie stared down into her mug, seemingly unable to meet Louise's eye. Setting the mug down, she stood up. 'I'm going to go back to Maternity and have a shower,' she muttered at last.

'All right, Rosie,' Louise said in a matter-of-fact sort of way. 'After that perhaps you'd like to come back and see Skye. You can visit her whenever you like, you know. And her father too, he could—'

'No,' said Rosie sharply. 'He won't come in here and I don't know that I want to see much of her either—there's no point, not if she's going to be adopted.'

Louise gave a sigh as she watched Rosie leave the room. It very much looked as if she would have to involve Social Services on this one, although for some reason at that precise moment she was loath to do so, hoping somehow that Baby Skye's future might be determined either by her own parents or, failing that, within Rosie's family.

She made her way back onto the ward here she found Matt talking to Nicky about Skye. They both looked up as Louise approached.

'How is she?' Louise glanced down into the incubator and saw that the baby was breathing with the help of a ventilator.

'She's struggling,' said Matt. 'But she's a little fighter—hopefully, she'll pull through.' He paused and looked over Louise's shoulder. 'The mother not with you?'

'No.' Louise shook her head. 'I think we're going to have problems there. She's very young—only sixteen. From what she's told me, it sounds as if she ran away from home some time ago and joined a group of travellers. She wasn't happy about the pregnancy, even considered termination, and now that baby has arrived early she's thinking adoption is the answer, presumably because the group she is with is ready to hit the road again.'

'Well, there's certainly no way this little poppet is going

to be fit to travel, not for a very long time,' said Matt, looking down at Skye. 'Does the mother have any family?'

'Ah,' said Louise, 'I'm working on that. Her parents live in Reading and she says she hasn't had any contact with them, neither does she want any, but, like I say, I'm working on it. I think the one thing we'll have to watch is that she doesn't simply disappear.'

'You mean with Skye?' asked Nicky in alarm.

'I don't think that's possible,' said Louise, 'not with the security we have in here. No, I was thinking more of Rosie herself. I know we haven't really any powers to stop her but she's in no fit state, either physically or mentally, to go anywhere at the moment.'

'What about the father in all this?' asked Matt as they moved away from Skye's incubator.

'Rosie was very vague about him,' admitted Louise. 'It didn't sound as if he wanted to know.'

'I wouldn't rule him out,' said Matt. 'He's probably only a lad himself, but you may well find he'll be more supportive than you think. Now, how's Baby Oliver this morning?'

'Come and have a look at him.' Louise led the way down the ward to Oliver Barrett's incubator, where Tracey was in the process of changing the baby's nappy, watched by Roma.

'Good morning.' Matt smiled and nodded at Tracey who, Louise noted, seemed to be looking more relaxed that morning. 'So how is this young man today?' He took the chart that Louise handed to him and began studying it. 'Well,' he said at last, 'I'm pleased to say he seems to be responding to the antibiotics for his infection. He still appears a little jaundiced so we'll continue with the photo-therapy, at least for the time being. What about his feeding, Sister?'

'All is well in that department, isn't it, Roma?' Louise turned to the nursery nurse.

'Yes,' Roma replied, passing wipes to Tracey who gently cleansed the baby's bottom. 'Tracey's been expressing her milk, he's feeding well and there's a slight weight gain.'

'Good.' Matt handed the chart back to Louise who replaced it on the hook at the end of the incubator. 'Keep up the good work.'

Baby Beth Cleaver was asleep, one tiny thumb in her mouth sucking furiously, so rather than disturb her, after reading through her notes and approving her progress, they moved on.

'I understand Gabrielle is coming back today from Intensive Care,' said Matt after they had seen the rest of the babies on the ward.

'Yes, I gather she's made excellent progress,' said Louise.

'It's still early days yet,' replied Matt. 'However, I think we can be quietly optimistic. Now, let me see how Lisa Kerrigan is coping with caring for Liam.'

'She's doing well,' said Louise as she led the way to the mothers' room. 'Almost ready to take him home now.'

The room smelt of baby powder and they found Lisa, having just bathed baby Liam, surrounded by the paraphernalia associated with bathing, dressing and feeding a tiny baby.

'I can't imagine ever getting anything else done when I get home,' said Lisa, looking up as they came into the room. 'It takes me all my time just caring for Liam.'

'You'll soon get used to it,' said Louise. 'Once you get home, you'll get into a daily routine.'

'Well, I hope so,' Lisa sighed, and began trying to secure the fastenings of a nappy on the tiny, squirming baby

on the changing mat before her. 'At least he's taking his
bottle well now, but every time I bath him my heart's in
my mouth—he's still so tiny, and so slippery...'

'You're doing fine,' said Matt encouragingly. 'Let me
have a look at him,' he added as Lisa finally secured the
nappy. Gently he lifted the baby and for a few moments,
watched by Lisa and Louise, cradled him in the crook of
his arm.

And suddenly, quite suddenly, overwhelmingly so,
Louise found she couldn't watch and had to turn away.
She wasn't sure why, she only knew that the sight of Matt
with that tiny baby settled so snugly and securely in his
arms and the look of tenderness on his face as he looked
down at him affected her profoundly. With a muttered
apology she slipped out of the room and headed back to
the comparative safety of her office.

There was to be little respite, however, for almost as
soon as she entered the room Nicky tapped on the door
and came in with a pile of folders requiring Louise's attention. 'Has Dr Forrester gone?' she asked, glancing
round the room almost as if she expected Matt to be hiding
somewhere.

'No.' In a concentrated effort to pull herself together
Louise shook her head. 'He's still with Lisa Kerrigan.'

'There isn't a problem with Liam, is there?' asked Nicky
anxiously.

'No, not at all. I think...I think Dr Forrester just wanted
to see Liam before he went, that's all.'

'He probably wanted to say goodbye,' said Nicky. 'He's
like that, isn't he?' She paused and threw Louise a searching glance, 'Actually,' she said, 'I hope you don't mind
me asking this, but I heard a rumour in the canteen yesterday and I wondered if it was true.'

'Oh, yes?' Louise braced herself, knowing what was

coming, knowing it had only been a matter of time. 'And what was that?'

'Well, there were some of the staff from Maternity in there,' said Nicky slowly, 'and someone was saying that you and Dr Forrester were once married. I said I thought they must be mistaken but they said they weren't. They were quite emphatic, actually. They said that you and he were married some while ago when you were working on Maternity and he was on Paediatrics.'

'Yes,' said Louise quietly, 'that is true.' When Nicky stared at her, apparently speechless, she went on, 'We did get married.'

'So are you still married or did you divorce?'

'No, we haven't divorced, not yet, but we are separated.'

'But your name, your name is Keating…'

'Keating is my maiden name,' said Louise. 'Everyone here at the hospital knew me as that. Somehow, it seemed easier to keep it.'

'Does anyone else know here on the unit?' asked Nicky at last.

'Michelle knows,' said Louise quietly, 'but I hadn't felt it necessary to tell anyone else because by the time I took up the post of Sister on this unit we had already separated and Matt…Dr Forrester had gone away. Maybe I should have said something when he came back to Ellie's…' she shrugged '…but I didn't really see the need, especially as we'll soon be divorcing anyway.'

'Oh, Louise, I'm so sorry.' Nicky stared at her. 'But whatever went wrong? He seems so nice…' She trailed off as if uncertain how to continue.

'He is,' agreed Louise. 'Shall we just say we shouldn't have got married in the first place…that it was a mistake?'

'But—'

'If you don't mind, Nicky, I really don't want to talk about it.'

'No, of course not.' While Nicky was looking as if she was desperately searching for what to say next, Michelle suddenly came into the office with a large parcel in her hands.

'Look at this,' she said. Then, as if she was suddenly aware of an atmosphere, she looked from Louise to Nicky and back to Louise again. 'I'm sorry,' she said. 'Am I interrupting something?'

'No,' said Louise briskly, 'not really. Nicky has just discovered my marital status, that's all.'

'Oh,' said Michelle, a guarded look coming into her eyes, 'Oh, I see.'

'It's all right,' Louise added, aware of the awkward silence. 'It wasn't exactly a state secret. Anyway, what have you got there, Michelle?' Deliberately changing the subject, she turned her attention to the parcel Michelle was carrying.

'Baby clothes,' said Michelle. After another anxious glance in Louise's direction, she placed the parcel on the desk and, watched by Louise and Nicky, proceeded to unwrap it. 'From Mrs Nesbitt,' she went on as she parted the last layers of tissue paper. 'She really is a treasure—just look at these.' They were the tiniest of garments, which at first glance one could be forgiven for thinking were dolls' clothes. Each was exquisitely worked—brushed cotton nightgowns, soft woollen matinée jackets with ribbon ties, tiny hats, bootees and mittens, mostly in white with the occasional coloured motif—a pink rosebud, a blue rabbit or a teddy bear.

'Oh, they're beautiful,' sighed Louise. 'She's so kind. So few people seem to do this sort of thing these days and, apart from doll's clothes, these little garments are almost impossible to buy.'

'Beth will look lovely in this,' said Nicky, holding up a little jacket with a delicate scalloped edging. 'I'll go and find Pauline.' Taking the jacket, she slipped out of the room. Louise suspected she was glad of the excuse to go.

'*I* didn't tell her,' said Michelle as the door closed behind Nicky.

'No, I know you didn't,' Louise replied with a little sigh. 'She said someone was gossiping about it in the canteen. It was inevitable, I suppose. Really, I guess, I should have said something when Matt came back, especially as so much of his work is on this unit. Well, it's out now.' She shrugged. 'And if it's common knowledge in the canteen then I dare say soon everyone will know.'

'Have you...have you done anything yet about divorce proceedings?' asked Michelle hesitantly.

Louise shook her head, 'No, we've decided to wait until...well, we've decided to wait, that's all.'

'You mean until after the wedding?' asked Michelle bluntly.

'Yes, something like that.' Louise took a deep breath. 'Now, tell me, are we all set for this hen night?'

'Yes, yes, we are.' Michelle's troubled expression cleared at the mention of her forthcoming hen night. 'There are eight of us—we're meeting at Angelo's first for a meal and a few drinks then we'll go into town and do a bit of clubbing.'

'Sounds great,' said Louise, 'Where are the guys going for their stag night?'

'Goodness knows—probably clubbing as well,' said Michelle with a grin as she left the office.

After a while Louise went back onto the ward where she found that Baby Gabrielle had just arrived in an incubator from the intensive care unit. The following half-hour was spent installing the little girl and making her comfortable. While Matt was examining Gabrielle and talking about her treatment to Russell and Julie, Louise saw Nicky beckoning to her to from further down the ward.

'What is it, Nicky?' asked Louise.

'You must go and take a look at Beth,' said Nicky. 'She looks absolutely adorable in Mrs Nesbitt's little jacket.'

Louise smiled and moved on to the corner of the room where Pauline Cleaver was feeding her baby girl. 'Doesn't she look lovely?' said Pauline, looking up as Louise approached. 'I don't think I've ever seen such wonderful knitwear.'

'It certainly seems to be a dying art,' agreed Louise.

'I used to do a lot of knitting myself at one time,' said Pauline. 'Nothing like this,' she hastened to add, 'just plain stuff really. When I was expecting my first two I did quite a bit for them and for the other one, of course...' She trailed off and Louise saw that her eyes had filled with tears.

'The other one?' said Louise gently.

'Yes, I lost one,' said Pauline. 'I had a miscarriage. But, do you know, I really mourn that little one. People tend to think because I didn't go very far in the pregnancy that somehow it didn't count, that it wasn't a real baby—but they don't understand. It was to me and to Malcolm.' She wiped the tears away with the back of her hand then gazed down at the baby in her lap, who stared back at her with wide, trusting eyes.

'I understand, Pauline,' said Louise softly.

Pauline shook her head sadly. 'No,' she said, 'not really. No one does, not unless they've been in the same situation themselves.' When Louise didn't answer Pauline looked up at her. 'Have you?' she said at last, her eyes widening. 'Have you been there, Sister?'

'Yes, Pauline,' Louise heard herself say, 'I have. I lost a baby at nearly five months.'

'Then you do understand,' said Pauline softly.

Louise smiled and, after touching Beth lightly on the top of her head moved away.

Louise's conversation with Pauline had disturbed her and it was on her mind long after she had left the unit that day. It was something she could hardly bear to think about even now after all this time. It was something that, after it had happened, she had tried to shut out, to close a door on because it had been too painful to face. When it happened to anyone else, to one of her patients on Maternity, she advised counselling or therapy but she had been unable to follow her own advice, believing that for her the best and only antidote had been to throw herself into her work and carry on with her life almost as if it had never happened. Sometimes, in the small hours of the night, she would occasionally allow herself to wonder what would have happened if her baby had gone to full term and had lived, but it was a dangerous avenue of thought and one which was rapidly abandoned.

She had discovered she was pregnant after that glorious weekend she and Matt had spent in Brighton. At first she'd simply been unable to believe it—they had been so careful—but there was no denying the blue line on the test she used, which confirmed her suspicions. Matt had been on the point of leaving Ellie's at the time to go on to a hospital in Cardiff to continue with the next stage of his training. He'd been dumbfounded when she'd told him the news, but in the end he'd taken it rather differently than she'd thought he might.

'I'm not going to Cardiff,' he told her only a week after hearing the news.

'But you have to go.' She stared at him in amazement. 'It's crucial that you go.'

'I can postpone it.' He shrugged. 'It's not the end of the world and I can always go on another course later on. Besides, you need me here with you now.'

'But, Matt…' He dismissed her protests and secretly she was rather pleased. They talked about moving in together then realised it was totally impractical as Louise was sharing with Michelle and Matt was in doctors' accommodation.

It was Angelo who told them of the little house in the terrace next door that had just come onto the market. They went to look at it and were immediately captivated. The house was empty and it was a simple matter to arrange a mortgage. In no time at all they moved in and if Louise felt any misgivings about the situation, because deep down she knew this was not what Matt had wanted, she pushed them to the back of her mind and allowed herself to be caught up in the excitement of preparing for her baby.

But now, she thought as she began getting ready for Michelle's hen night, it was much too painful even to think about that time when she and Matt had been so happy, so with a determined effort she once again put it out of her mind, just as she had done so many times before.

She knew it was going to take a great effort that night to get into a celebratory mood as she really didn't even feel like going out, let alone going on into town after the meal to a club. But this was for Michelle and she and Michelle had been friends for a long time so in Louise's mind there was no question that she should make this effort.

In her wardrobe Louise found a silky skirt in a scarlet

and white print, which she teamed with a matching scarlet sequinned top and a pair of strappy, high-heeled shoes. Her hair she tried in several styles—behind her ears, in front of her ears, caught up in a large grip on top of her head—but in the end she allowed it to fall freely around her face. Matt liked it that way, she thought as she sprayed herself with her favourite French perfume, then immediately she dismissed the thought. What did it matter now whether she wore her hair in the way he liked it or not? It was over between them and the sooner she got used to that the better.

If she was honest, this whole thing with him coming back to Ellie's had been far more difficult than she had ever imagined. Having him there right beside her each day on the unit and then him coming to the house had been far from easy. Maybe it would all be better once the wedding was over and their own divorce proceedings could get under way. Once the house was sold and everything was divided between them they could perhaps go back to the way they had been before they had even met. Yes, she told herself firmly as she picked up her bag and her jacket, of course things would be better then.

So if that was the case, why did she get this sinking feeling in the pit of her stomach every time she thought about it? Why did her heart leap whenever she unexpectedly caught sight of Matt and why did she find herself looking for him every day on the unit and just waiting for the moment when he arrived? Deep in her heart she knew it was because there was no way that things could ever go back to the way they had been, because now she knew what it was like to have loved and to have been loved by Matt Forrester, and after that there was no way things could ever return to the way they had been before.

CHAPTER SEVEN

THERE was a festive atmosphere in Angelo's that night and it was obvious that the Italian couple had pulled out all the stops for Michelle's hen night. As the women arrived, Maria and Angelo produced specially prepared cocktails designed to get the evening off to a good start, and by the time they had all ordered their favourite pasta dishes Louise felt herself begin to relax.

One of the women in the party was Michelle's cousin Hayley, another an old schoolfriend but the rest, including Nicky and Roma from SCBU, were staff from Ellie's who, with the exception of one, Louise knew.

'Louise, have you met Tina?' asked Michelle, leaning forward from her place further down the table.

'No, I don't believe I have.' Louise shook her head.

The woman, a vivacious brunette, smiled and waved. 'I'm new to Ellie's. Tina Gordon—Staff on Ortho.'

'Hi, Tina. Louise Keating—Sister on special care baby unit.' Louise waved back.

A little later the food began to arrive, served by Maria and her younger sister Anona. It was as delicious as ever and everyone tucked enthusiastically into the cannelloni, tagliatelle or gnocchi, each served with Angelo's own mouth-watering sauces. Michelle was on top form that night and looked ravishing in a black dress that perfectly complemented her auburn hair and creamy complexion. Her eyes sparkled and, surrounded by her friends, she appeared animated and happy.

Louise hadn't had a hen night before she'd married

Matt. In fact, there had been no time for much preparation at all and sometimes, even now, she wondered whether the whole thing had been little more than an impulsive reaction to circumstances.

But she didn't want to start thinking about that now, not tonight. This was Michelle's night and the last thing Louise wanted was to start comparing this to her own situation.

It was after they'd finished the main course, while they were waiting for Maria to bring Angelo's wonderful selection of ice creams that there was one of those lulls in conversation which was broken eventually by Tina who looked round the table at the others. 'I say,' she said, her cheeks flushed and her eyes sparkling, 'have you seen that gorgeous new reg on Paediatrics? Who is he? Does anyone know anything about him?'

In the silence that followed, Louise imagined that everyone was looking at her as if waiting for her to explain. She opened her mouth but nothing came out, and in the end it was Michelle who came to her rescue.

'That will be Matt Forrester you're talking about,' she said.

'Matt... Mmm, is that his name? I like that, it suits him.' Tina nodded. 'I have to say I reckon I'm in with a chance there. Whenever I've seen him around the hospital I've caught his eye, so to speak. So, is he free?' Another silence followed her question and she looked round at the others. 'What?' she said at last.

'Well...it's just that...' Michelle began.

'Don't tell me—he's got someone, is that it?' Tina sighed. 'Not that I'm surprised. Someone as gorgeous as that was never going to be unattached.'

'Actually,' said Nicky frostily, 'Matt Forrester is married.'

'Now, why doesn't that surprise me?' Tina gave a short bitter laugh. 'The best ones always are. Story of my life really. Some hunky chap gives me the eye and he turns out to be married. Do we know who she is?'

It was at that point that Tina seemed to become aware of the awkwardness amongst some of the others seated around the table. 'What's wrong?' she demanded at last, looking round at the others. 'Have I said something?'

Louise took a deep breath, something telling her that it was only she who could answer the question. 'It's all right, Tina,' she said at last. 'It's nothing you've said, really. It's just that I'm married to Matt Forrester.'

'You!' Tina's mouth fell open. 'Oh, God, why didn't someone say? Why did you all let me go on like that? I feel such a fool now…'

'Don't,' said Louise lightly. 'There's no need, believe me. You weren't to know.'

'But all that about him giving me the eye…'

'He may well have done,' Louise went on calmly. 'You see, we're separated.'

'Oh…' Tina stared at her. 'Oh,' she said again, 'I see.'

'So who knows,' said Hayley from further down the table, 'you could well be in with a chance after all.'

A ripple of laughter spread around the table but Louise was aware that Michelle threw her an anxious glance. She was saved from any further embarrassment by the arrival of Maria and Anona with trays laden with glass dishes of Italian ice cream of every flavour and colour imaginable, and the moment was lost in the general cries of delight and dire mutterings about calories and weight control.

The incident had upset Louise, however, and it played on her mind for the rest of the time they were at Angelo's. She wasn't sure why, because deep down she knew she would have to get used to other women showing interest in Matt, especially after their divorce was over, but the incident with Tina had bothered her just as the fact that Matt had spent Christmas with a Scottish radiologist had bothered her.

It shouldn't bother her, so why had it? Was she jealous? she asked herself a little later as they all poured out of Angelo's and into a couple of mini-cabs. Of course she wasn't jealous. How could she be jealous? She and Matt had been a mistake. They had both recognised that fact, were doing something about it and moving on. So why did she feel so miserable about it?

'Are you all right, Lou?' asked Michelle anxiously. They were seated in the back of one of the mini-cabs, together with Hayley, while Nicky was in the front seat beside the driver.

'Yes,' she lied. 'I'm fine.'

'That's all right, then,' said Michelle with a little sigh of relief. 'I was beginning to wonder if all this was getting to you—under the circumstances, I mean.'

'Of course not,' said Louise firmly. 'I'm having a wonderful time.'

From that moment onwards she made a superhuman attempt to have fun, to let Michelle at least think she was enjoying every moment.

'Good evening, ladies.' One of the club bouncers nodded as a little later they all tumbled out of the mini-cabs. 'Looks like you're all up for a good time.'

Laughing and giggling, they made their way down the stairs to the huge basement of the building. It was almost midnight and the club was heaving with what seemed like thousands of jumping, gyrating figures beneath the flashing strobe lighting while the impact of the music was like a physical assault on the eardrums.

'Oh, my God!' said Roma. The oldest of the group, she

paused for a moment on the stairs, gazing at the scene with her hands to her mouth. 'This is really not my thing—I'm not sure I can cope.'

'Yes, you can!' cried Tina. 'Come on—let's party!'

Louise and Nicky made their way to the bar where they bought champagne and took it in ice buckets back to the others, who had found a table in an alcove. Gradually, no doubt aided by the champagne and the couple of cocktails she'd had at Angelo's, Louise felt herself relax and along with the rest of the girls was soon helpless with laughter at the most trivial of incidents. Eventually, in spite of reservations from at least three of the group, they all found themselves flocking onto the dance floor where they happily boogied the rest of the night away.

The night was almost over and the tempo of the music had changed from the pounding repetitive rhythm that Louise was convinced she would hear in her head for at least the next week to a slower, throbbing beat, presumably for the benefit of those clubbers who had actually come with a partner or who had met one during the course of the evening. Dancers began leaving the floor in droves while others crowded on and somehow, in the crush, Louise became separated from the others. As she began to fight her way through the mass of people she suddenly felt someone's arms go around her, drawing her back into the midst of the crowd on the floor. Instinctively she began to struggle.

'It's all right,' the person said urgently but reassuringly in her ear, 'it's me.'

'Matt?' She turned her head in bewilderment.

'Yes. Shh!' Putting his finger to his lips, he gathered her into his arms. 'Come on.'

She felt too weak to offer any resistance, probably because of what she'd had to drink and unable, in the crush, to push him away. Then she realised, as his arms tightened around her and she felt the roughness of his cheek against her own, that really she didn't want to push him away.

It felt incredibly good to be close to Matt again after all this time, to smell him, the familiar scent of the aftershave he used, together with the essence that was quite simply Matt himself. For a while it was as if they were entirely alone, that the mass of humanity around them had ceased to exist as they held each other and moved gently, not even in time to the music which, in spite of being slower than it had been, was still fast and somewhat furious.

He moved his head, bending it slightly against her, and as she lifted her face his mouth sought hers, his lips warm and urgent but at the same time just as tender as they had ever been.

I must be drunk, Louise thought. How else could this be happening? Probably Matt was drunk as well. Maybe that was their excuse, that this wouldn't be happening if they were both stone cold sober. But she was enjoying it, enjoying it so very much—would she have enjoyed it if she were sober? She didn't know and at that moment, as the music throbbed and pounded and they clung together, neither did she care. She had missed this, had missed him so much, and here he was now and once more she was in his arms. For the moment nothing else mattered—not the fact that they were in the midst of thousands of young clubbers, that their friends were somewhere in the same building or that in just over a week's time they would be setting in motion the wheels that would bring their sham of a marriage to a close.

At that moment she would have been quite content to remain there forever but, of course, that could not be and all too soon the music faded slightly, Matt moved and without a word managed to steer the pair of them to the edge of the floor then through the crush of people into a bar marginally quieter than the rest of the club.

'I didn't know you were here,' she said.

'We've only been here about half an hour,' Matt replied. 'We saw you but Andy said best not to let on. I think he was afraid Michelle would think he was spying on her. Apparently there was a bit of a fuss at work—one of the paramedics had told Michelle he would give her a night to remember tonight. Andy got annoyed about it and Michelle accused him of not trusting her.'

'I haven't heard anything about that,' said Louise.

'Anyway, we're about to move on,' said Matt with a rueful smile. 'I saw you on the floor and I wanted a dance before we went—you didn't mind, did you?'

'Of course not.' She looked at him and their eyes met.

'Louise…' he began, 'I—'

'I must get back to the others,' she said, suddenly unable to cope with what she saw in his eyes. 'They'll be wondering where I've got to.'

'Me, too.' He gave a reluctant smile. 'I'd better go and make sure Andy doesn't get completely paralytic.'

Then he was gone, swallowed up by the crowd, leaving her to fight her way back to the far side of the club, only to find that far from having missed her the others had been more than entertained.

'What's going on?' she asked Nicky.

'Oh, Louise, where were you?' demanded Nicky helplessly. 'You've missed all the fun. It was Ronnie—you know Ronnie, he's a paramedic—and a couple of his mates. They'd dressed up as women and did a strip. Two of them have beards—I've never seen anything so funny in all my life. It seems Ronnie had promised Michelle a night to remember.'

'And I'll certainly never forget that,' said Michelle, wiping the tears of laughter that were running down her cheeks. 'Didn't you see it, Lou?'

'No, I didn't.' Louise shook her head. 'I er...I saw someone I knew...'

They left soon after that and the mini-cabs took them home where Louise was happy simply to fall into bed.

She slept soundly and deeply for several hours, awaking to bright sunlight, the sound of church bells and the cacophony of ducks on the river below her window.

After making tea, she went back to bed and took the Sunday papers with her, allowing herself the luxury of a lie-in. She had imagined she might feel dreadful that morning after the late night meal, the greater than usual quantity of alcohol and the pounding music, but apart from a slight ringing in her ears she was surprised to find that she felt amazingly good. She was a bit tired, but that wasn't really surprising—she very often was tired after an intense week on SCBU. But this morning, for some reason, she had that good-to-be-alive feeling, along with an added sense of excitement. Why that should be she didn't really know. She was looking forward to Michelle's wedding at the end of the week, but she doubted it could only be that which was responsible for this unusually heightened sense of well-being.

So what was it? She frowned as she lay back against her pillows and turned the pages of the paper, not really taking in what she was reading. Could it be anything to do with Matt turning up the way he had? It had been a surprise certainly, and she had to confess she had enjoyed dancing with him. He'd kissed her as well—hadn't he? Or had she imagined that? No, he had kissed her, she was pretty sure, but no doubt he'd been drunk. She'd certainly had more to drink than she should have done. Probably it shouldn't have happened but, what the hell, they weren't divorced yet and if you couldn't kiss your own husband at your best friend's hen night then it was a pretty poor show. But could it really be only that that was making her feel so good this morning?

The ringing of the telephone on her bedside table broke into her thoughts. 'Hello?' she said, lifting the receiver and expecting it to be Michelle or maybe Nicky wanting an inquest on the night before.

'Louise?'

Her fingers tightened involuntarily around the phone. 'Matt?' she said.

'Are you OK?'

'Of course.' Had he thought she'd been so far gone the night before that he considered it necessary to check up on her?

'You got home all right then?'

'Oh, yes. Did you?' she added.

'Eventually.'

'And are you the worse for wear this morning?'

'No, I'm not too bad,' he replied. 'A bit fragile, that's all. I felt responsible for Andy and I'd promised Michelle I'd keep an eye on him.'

'Probably just as well.' She paused. 'By the way, Ronnie and his paramedic friends turned up while you and I were…dancing.'

'Really? Was there any trouble?'

'No.' She chuckled. 'It appears they arrived in drag and then did a strip—that was what Ronnie had meant about giving Michelle a night to remember.'

'I see.' Matt also chuckled. 'Well, maybe it was just as well that Andy wasn't around.'

'Yes, you're probably right.'

'Louise…'

'Yes?'

'About last night…'

'Don't worry about it, Matt.'

'No?'

'No, it was just one of those things, that's all. We'd both had a bit to drink. It probably shouldn't have happened, but it did. There was no harm done.'

'OK.' He paused. 'Louise…'

'Yes, Matt?'

'I was just wondering…' he said. 'What are you doing today?' Not giving her a chance to answer, he went on, 'I thought perhaps we could have lunch somewhere together…'

'Sorry, Matt, I can't,' she said quickly. 'I've some decorating to do.'

'Decorating?' She could hear the amazement in his voice.

'Yes, the kitchen needs a coat of emulsion.'

'And you have to do that today—on your day off?' He sounded incredulous now.

'When else would I do it? It has to be done, especially as the house is going on the market.'

'Couldn't you get someone in to do it?'

'Have you any idea what they charge?' she protested. 'No, I'll do it myself. It won't take long, it's not that big an area.'

'No, I suppose not…'

'I'll see you at work tomorrow.'

'Yes, all right, Louise. Bye.'

'Bye, Matt.' She replaced the receiver and leaned back against the pillows. It was quite true what she had told Matt—the kitchen walls did need a coat of emulsion and it really did need doing before the house went on the market. But Matt's offer of lunch had been very tempting and if it had been anyone else she would probably have allowed herself to have been talked out of a day's decorating.

Why had she turned him down? She knew it had something to do with the night before, of how she had felt, being in his arms again, but at the same time she also knew it was more to do with the fact that they had both just more or less agreed that what had happened had been a result of the drink or the atmosphere in the club, and had been a mistake—just like their marriage. With a deep sigh Louise closed her eyes.

Their marriage. It had seemed almost inevitable at the time—they loved each other, she was pregnant and they had found the perfect little house in which to live.

'We may as well get married.' Matt had said it quite casually one evening.

'But I thought we'd agreed not to, that marriage was something neither of us wanted,' she'd replied in surprise.

'That was then. Things have changed now.'

'You mean because of the baby?'

'Yes, I suppose so, partly,' he'd agreed. 'We are going to be parents now, Louise, and that carries a lot of responsibility. I know it may seem old-fashioned these days but I don't like the idea of children born out of wedlock...'

'I didn't know you felt that way, Matt.' She'd been surprised but at the same time strangely moved by his convictions.

'It's probably all down to my upbringing,' he'd said. 'Listening to too many of my father's sermons on Sunday mornings, I expect.'

Whatever it was, it resulted in Matt booking the local register office for one Saturday morning. They had told no one except Michelle and Andy who agreed to act as witnesses. They only told their families afterwards when they announced their marriage, along with the fact that Louise was expecting a baby.

She wore an ankle-length dress of old rose crushed velvet with tiny crystal beads in her hair and carried a small posy of pink rosebuds. Matt wore his grey suit—the only suit he possessed—Andy took a few photographs and afterwards they went to Angelo's for a celebratory meal. Maria cried when she learnt why they were there and Angelo produced a bottle of champagne.

'What about a honeymoon?' Michelle said. 'You must have a honeymoon even if it's only for one night. You must go somewhere.' So they went back to Brighton—to the same hotel where they had gone before. And they were happy. Weren't they?

Louise frowned now as she thought about it. There had been so much misery since it was difficult to remember but, yes, they had been happy then, when they had exchanged their vows, afterwards at Angelo's and later at Brighton, certainly at Brighton. It maybe hadn't been what they might have wanted, not what they might have planned if the circumstances had been different, but they had been happy. Until it had all started to go wrong, until it had all fallen apart.

With a sigh she sat up in bed, pushed the papers away then moving to the edge of the bed, stood up and padded to the bathroom. It was no good lying there going over what had gone wrong, endlessly speculating over whether or not they could have put things right. After a shower, she went to the kitchen, poured orange juice, made some toast and put coffee on to percolate.

It was true what she had told Matt, she thought as she sat at the table and gazed round at the tiny kitchen. The walls really had taken on a dingy tone of late and were badly in need of a fresh coat of paint. She had already bought the paint and the tin stood in the corner together with a roller and paint tray, just waiting for her to get on with the job. Until that moment she had been quite looking forward to it. She'd done decorating in the past—when she and Matt had first moved into the house—and she had enjoyed it then but now, quite suddenly, since talking to Matt, she found she had lost all enthusiasm.

After clearing away the breakfast dishes, she covered the kitchen units with some dustsheets then changed into her oldest pair of jeans and one of Matt's shirts that she found in a charity bag. Fortifying herself by pouring a second mug of coffee, she prised the lid from the tin of paint, stirred it thoroughly and had just poured some into the tray when the doorbell sounded.

With a muttered exclamation she set down the tin, smearing her hands with paint as she did so. She stood up and hurried to the front door, wiping her hands down the sides of her shirt then pushing a stray strand of hair behind one ear. If she was honest, she was annoyed by the interruption—whoever it was on a Sunday morning, be it a neighbour or a friend from the hospital, would expect to be asked inside and given coffee which, no doubt, would delay her for a good hour.

In growing irritation she pulled open the door. Matt stood on the doorstep, a large brown paper carrier in his arms. She stared at him in amazement.

'This is getting to be a habit,' he said.

'What is?'

'This.' He stretched out one hand and smoothed her cheek. She took a step backwards and he grinned. 'Last time you were gardening and it was dirt—this time it's paint.'

'Oh.' Louise put one hand up to her face where he had

touched it. 'Have I got it on my face? I was just pouring it into the tray when I heard the doorbell...'

'Aren't you going to ask me in?' he said.

'Well...'

'I know you said you were going to be busy—too busy to go out to lunch—so I've brought lunch with me.' He glanced down at the bag.

'I'm still busy...' she began.

'Yes, I know,' he said. 'That's why I've come to help.'

'You...you've come to help?' She stared at him.

'Yes.'

'But why?'

'It's the least I can do. After all, this is still half my house and I will benefit from its sale as much as you.'

She stood aside and Matt brushed past her into the hall. 'I say,' he said lifting his head, 'is that coffee I smell?'

'Yes,' she replied weakly, 'it is.'

'And isn't that my shirt you're wearing?' he added as he turned to face her, his eyes twinkling. 'I'd wondered what had happened to it.'

Louise smiled. Closing the door behind him she followed him into the kitchen.

CHAPTER EIGHT

'So AN airlift is being arranged for later today for Baby
Holmes to take him to a neurological unit.' Louise looked
round at her assembled staff as they received the report on
that day's patients.

'You said he'd suffered a brain haemorrhage?' Student
Nurse Chrissie Watkins looked quite stricken. 'Can he possibly survive that?' Chrissie was new to the unit and was
still at the stage where she was constantly amazed at just
how much could be done for the premature babies in their
care.

'Of course,' Louise replied briskly. 'The risk is far
greater, of course, but we have had babies that have gone
off to other units after suffering a haemorrhage and have
then been returned to us here until they are well enough
to go home.'

'But don't they suffer brain damage?' persisted Chrissie.

'Inevitably, yes, some of them do,' Louise said sadly,
'and that is one of the risks unfortunately that we constantly face with the babies in our care.' She paused. 'Now,
if we can move on, please. As you know, we have three
new admissions to the ward this morning so it will be an
extremely busy day. Mr Richardson and Dr Forrester will
be along shortly to see the new babies. Gabrielle continues
to improve, although I see from the notes that she had
difficulty feeding yesterday so I'll be asking one of them
to take a look at her.'

'What's happening with Skye?' asked Roma, looking up
from the pad on which she was taking notes.

'She's still very poorly,' Louise replied. 'I've also had word to say that Maternity had to involve Social Services as there have been all sorts of problems with Rosie over the weekend.'

'What sort of problems?' asked Michelle. 'Do we know?'

'Well, as I predicted, she tried to leave the unit,' replied Louise. 'She was intercepted, however, and brought back, but only because she still needed medical attention herself. We won't be able to keep her for much longer—a couple of days at the most—but already she's saying she doesn't want to see Skye again.'

'Then what?' asked Roma.

'She says she intends joining her travelling friends on the road.'

'But what about Skye?'

'Well, this is why Social Services have to be involved,' said Louise. 'Rosie's considering adoption, but that can take time. Presumably if she just leaves her daughter here, Skye will eventually end up in care.'

'And if Rosie decides to stay, to let her friends go without her?'

'She'll probably have to go into a hostel until the council can find her suitable accommodation, unless, of course, she can be persuaded to contact her parents.'

'It's a pretty desperate situation, isn't it?' said Michelle slowly.

'It is, yes,' Louise replied, 'but we mustn't lose sight of the fact that our job is primarily to care for Skye until she's strong enough to leave this unit. Right.' She glanced around at her staff. 'If there aren't any more questions, can we get on please?'

Amidst rustlings and murmurings the staff stood up and began to make their way onto the ward to take up their various tasks. Only Michelle hung back for a moment. 'How were you yesterday?' she asked Louise with a rueful smile.

'Not too bad,' said Louise. 'How about you—did you have a hangover?'

'You could say that,' said Michelle. 'My head was thumping until the middle of the afternoon. Mind you, I think it was as much the music as the alcohol. Do you know, I could hear that music all day? Poor old Roma reckons she'll be permanently deaf.'

'I know what you mean,' Louise replied with a laugh. 'It was a good night, though, wasn't it?'

'Excellent,' said Michelle. 'I had a wonderful time.'

'Have you seen Andy?'

'Yes, he crawled round yesterday afternoon. Sounds like they had a good time as well. Do you know, they were actually in that club at the same time as we were at one point before they moved on to the next one?'

'Really?' said Louise, feigning surprise. 'Mind you, there were a few thousand there...'

'I have to say I didn't get much done yesterday,' said Michelle as they moved onto the ward, 'which just goes to show that there's something to be said for not having stag and hen nights the night before one's wedding.'

'Oh, absolutely,' Louise replied, then found herself wondering what her friend would think if she knew what had taken place on the dance floor between herself and Matt.

'How about you?' asked Michelle.

'Me?' Startled, she looked up.

'Yes, did you get much done yesterday?'

'Oh, that. Yes, I did, as a matter of fact. I decorated the kitchen.'

'You did what?' Michelle looked astounded. 'What, all on your own?'

'Er, no, actually, Matt gave me a hand.'

'Well, well—is that a fact?' Michelle's eyes widened speculatively. 'You must tell me more later.'

'Nothing to tell, really,' said Louise with a shrug. 'The kitchen needed decorating and Matt just happened to phone...'

But Michelle had moved away down the ward and although she had a little smile on her face she was no longer listening to what Louise was saying.

Louise watched her in slight exasperation. She didn't want Michelle reading anything into the fact that Matt had helped her the day before, she really would have to set the matter right later. But for the moment she had work to do and she was forced to put the matter out of her mind.

The next half-hour was spent finalising the arrangements for the baby who needed to be airlifted to the neurological unit at a hospital sixty miles away. Louise had to liaise with staff on the unit, giving precise details of Baby William Holmes's condition, and also with the special air team who were to accompany him, after which she spent a further half-hour talking to William's distraught parents, trying to reassure them that everything possible was being done in the battle for their tiny son's life.

Finally leaving the parents in the relatives' room, Louise came onto the ward to meet Neil and Matt for their ward round.

'You have a full house this morning, Sister Keating,' said Neil as he glanced through the pile of notes.

'Yes, indeed.' Louise said, and without even looking at him, suddenly very much aware of Matt by her side, went on, 'Three new admissions in twenty-four hours is high.'

'Baby Kerrigan has gone home, I presume?' asked the consultant.

'Yes. And Baby Holmes is being moved later today. I'd like you to take a look at him, please, and maybe have another word with his parents.'

'Of course. Any other problems?' Neil looked at Louise over the top of his glasses.

'Baby Bradley is still very poorly.'

'And Gabrielle Fox?'

'Actually, she's doing very well.'

'Good, well, I think first we'll take a look at baby Holmes.'

As they moved onto the ward Matt moved a little closer to Louise. 'No ill effects?' he murmured.

'Ill effects?' she said softly. 'From what?'

'Well, decorating, of course,' he replied.

'Oh, that,' she said lightly. 'No, of course not. It would take more than a spot of decorating to get the better of me.'

'What did you think I meant?' he murmured softly. By this time they had reached William's incubator and Louise chose to ignore Matt's question, turning her attentions instead to the baby whose breathing was assisted by a ventilator and whose tiny form was attached to a heart monitor. In one corner of the incubator, amongst the awesome array of tubes issuing lifesaving drugs to assist in the baby's desperate struggle for survival, someone had placed a small fluffy blue rabbit.

The ward round that morning took over an hour and a half, as Louise had suspected it might, and by the time the doctors finally left the unit she felt quite drained. There was to be no respite, however, as there was a problem with William's ventilator and Matt had to be sent for to deal with it. After he had gone, Louise was caught up with one administrative task after another involving dozens of phone calls and e-mails.

'Coming for a break?' Michelle looked round the office door just after midday.

'I'm not sure that I can.' Louise looked at the mountain of paperwork on her desk requiring her attention.

'Just ten minutes,' Michelle persisted. 'It'll do you good.'

'Oh, all right.' Louise stood up and stretched then with a little sigh followed Michelle out of the unit and into the staff room.

'So, what's all this about decorating?' Michelle took a couple of cans of fruit juice from the cool cabinet and passed one to Louise as they both collapsed into a couple of easy chairs.

'It had to be done,' Louise replied warily. Already she had the feeling that this break wasn't entirely because Michelle thought she needed it.

'So why the urgency? Couldn't it wait until you weren't suffering from a hangover?'

'Actually, I didn't really have a hangover,' Louise admitted, pulling the ring on her can of juice. 'But the kitchen had to be done because the house is going on the market.'

'Oh, Lou, no.' Michelle stared at her, her own can of drink poised inches from her mouth.

'I can't stay there, Michelle. I won't be able to afford it.'

'But you've been OK, haven't you?'

'Until now, yes,' Louise replied, 'but only because Matt has gone on paying his share of the mortgage. I can't expect him to do that forever and the value of the property has risen so steeply that I haven't a hope of buying him out.'

'Does it really have to come to this?'

'I'm afraid it does. We'll be instructing solicitors very soon now.'

'Oh, Louise.' Michelle's eyes looked quite moist as she stared at her. 'I really had hoped that things might be different, that you both might reconsider, especially after Matt came back...'

'I told you at the time there was no chance of that.' Louise took a mouthful of juice.

'Yes, yes, I know you did,' Michelle persisted, 'but since Matt has been back you seem so...'

'So what?' Louise raised her eyebrows.

'I don't know. So...' Michelle struggled to find the word she needed. 'So together somehow,' she said at last. 'So right. And then after...well, after Saturday night.'

'What about Saturday night?' Louise threw Michelle a sharp glance, wondering to what she was referring. Michelle had been nowhere near the dance floor when she and Matt...so she couldn't possibly have seen...

'Oh, nothing.' Michelle coloured slightly.

'No, go on, you can't leave it there. What about Saturday night?' Louise insisted.

'I said I wouldn't say,' muttered Michelle, 'but, oh, well, all right, then, but don't let on that I told you, will you?'

'That you told me what?'

'It was Roma—just now in the sluice. She said...'

'She said what?' Louise lowered her can.

'That she was on her way back from the loo on Saturday night when she saw you and Matt on the dance floor.'

'Really?' said Louise coolly. 'What else did she say?'

'That you were...well, that you looked very intimate.'

'Were those her exact words?' asked Louise in the same cool tone.

'Er, no,' Michelle admitted. 'Actually, she said you were snogging away like a couple of teenagers.'

'We were *not* snogging!' protested Louise indignantly.

'No?' Michelle raised her eyebrows. 'So what was it that Roma saw, then?'

'Well, we had a dance, that's all.'

'Oh, so you did see Matt there, then.'

'Yes, I did.'

'It's just that you didn't say…' Michelle protested.

'Didn't say what?' demanded Louise.

'That you'd seen the guys. Earlier, when I said that Andy had told me that they were at the club at the same time that we were, you didn't say that you knew. If you'd known, I would have thought you might have done.'

'I didn't see Andy.'

'Just Matt.'

'Yes, just Matt.'

'And you just had a dance with Matt, nothing more?'

'We may have had a little kiss—just for old times' sake. You know what it's like—we'd both had a drink and in that atmosphere…' Louise shrugged then in sudden exasperation she said, 'Anyway, what is this, Michelle, the third degree?'

'Sorry, Lou.' Michelle had the grace to look a little shamefaced. 'It's just that I can hardly bear the fact that you and Matt are splitting up, especially at a time when Andy and I are so happy.'

'I guess that's life,' said Louise briskly. 'These things happen and we don't always have control over how or when they happen—they just do.'

'I know,' Michelle gulped. 'I suppose it's just that it all seems so unnecessary somehow…because, well, as I said, you and Matt seem so right together and I don't think I'll ever understand why you can't make a go of things…not in a million years I won't.'

Louise was silent for a moment then, taking a deep breath, she looked across the small coffee-table at her friend. 'I told you before, Michelle,' she said, 'Matt and I should never have got married.'

'I know you keep saying that.' It was Michelle's turn to sound exasperated. 'But the fact is, you *did* get married. You *are* married.'

'I know,' agreed Louise calmly, determined not to allow herself to get ruffled, 'but it was a mistake. We both know that.'

'But surely—'

'No. Listen, Michelle, I know you mean well, but it's no use going on about it. The truth of the matter is, Matt and I never had any intentions of getting married until I found…I was pregnant. That was the only reason we got married.'

'The *only* reason?' Michelle's voice rose slightly. 'What about love? Didn't you love each other then?'

'Well, yes, I suppose we did.' Louise was a little taken aback by her friend's bluntness. 'Yes, we did, but I guess it wasn't enough for us to start thinking about changing things and certainly not about spending the rest of our lives together. You're forgetting, Michelle, we really hadn't known each other for very long. My getting pregnant was a disastrous mistake.'

'But Matt stood by you, didn't he?'

'Yes, he did,' Louise agreed quietly.

'He could have just left you, gone off and got on with his life, his career…'

'This is Matt we're talking about,' said Louise dryly. 'Matt was never one to shirk his responsibilities.'

'But once you were married...surely then it changed things between you?'

Louise shrugged. 'Right from the start I think Matt wondered what he had done, especially when his career seemed to grind to a halt because of the training post he'd turned down. I knew he was bitterly disappointed and I sensed that he resented the fact that he had felt obliged to marry me.'

'I'm sure he never felt that way,' said Michelle, shaking her head. 'And besides, he should have taken responsibility the same as you had to. Even in today's climate with all the methods of contraception people should be aware that they may have to pay a price for sex...that there could be a baby at the end of it.'

'Yes, I agree with you. But there wasn't, was there?' said Louise.

'Wasn't what?' Michelle frowned as if she had lost her train of thought.

'There wasn't a baby.' To her horror Louise felt a lump rise in her throat.

'No, I know there wasn't, Lou,' said Michelle with a sigh. 'And whatever you might think, Matt was very upset about that.'

'Yes, I know he was,' Louise said, blinking furiously, not wanting Michelle to see the tears that were unexpectedly, dangerously close, 'but afterwards, once we'd got over it, he regretted the fact that we had married.'

'Louise, no!' Michelle looked shocked. 'I'm sure you're wrong.'

Louise shrugged. 'Well, let's face it, by then we were back to square one, weren't we? We had married because of the baby and once the baby was no longer there...'

'I still think you're wrong.'

'So how do explain the fact that we started arguing around that time?' said Louise.

'Well, all couples argue,' protested Michelle. 'Me and Andy argue...but what sort of things did you argue about?'

'His career, my career...everything...but mainly our careers.' Louise made a dismissive gesture. 'I knew he resented the fact that he hadn't gone to Cardiff when he had the chance, that if we hadn't got married... Anyway...' She took a deep breath, completely in control of her feelings again. 'By the time the training post in Scotland came up things were pretty bad between us. I told him to go and I think he was glad to do so.'

'Oh, Lou, I still think it's so sad,' said Michelle.

'Yes, well...' Louise was saved from any further awkwardness as the staff room door was suddenly pushed open and Nicky appeared. She paused for a moment in the doorway, looking from one to the other of them as if she sensed some sort of tension between them. 'I'm sorry to interrupt,' she said, 'but Rosie has just come onto the unit. She's saying now that she does want to see Skye again. I thought you would want to know, Louise.'

'Right, yes, of course.' Briskly Louise stood up, glad of the opportunity to return to the demands of her professional life and to be able to push her emotional problems to the back of her mind where they belonged. 'Thanks, Nicky, I'll come right away. It looks like Rosie might be having a change of heart, then?'

'It seems that way, yes.' Nicky nodded then when Michelle remained where she was she threw her a curious glance. 'You all right, Michelle?' she said.

'Yes, fine,' Michelle said. 'I'll be back in a few minutes.'

Together Louise and Nicky returned to the ward where they found Rosie sitting outside the office. She was dressed today in a long, dark green, cotton skirt, a loose top of the same material and a pair of black, clumpy-looking leather boots. Her hair she had braided into dozens of tiny plaits and around her neck and her wrists she wore numerous bands, some of silver, others of leather.

'Hello, Rosie.' Louise stopped in front of her, looking down at the rather forlorn-looking figure.

'I want to see her,' said Rosie abruptly.

'Very well, Rosie, of course you can,' Louise replied. 'I told you, you could come and see Skye whenever you like. Come on, let's go and get your hands scrubbed then you can come and see her.'

'My hands aren't dirty!' protested Rosie.

'Neither are mine,' said Louise, 'but I'm still going to wash them before I go near any of the babies. I've been out of the ward and I could have touched something that's covered in germs. Just think how dreadful it would be if I passed those germs on to Skye or to any one of those other tiny babies in my care. None of them have the strength to fight off colds, or flu, or tummy bugs.'

In silence Rosie followed Louise into the sluice. 'I suppose you heard about yesterday,' she said a moment later, casting Louise a sidelong glance as they both lathered their hands.

'What about yesterday?' said Louise lightly, feeling it best she heard this from Rosie herself, instead of letting the girl think everyone had been talking about her behind her back.

'I was going to go.'

'Were you? Where were you going to go?'

'Back to the site,' said Rosie sullenly, 'but then I wasn't well and when I was back in the ward Mitzi came to see me.'

'Who's Mitzi?' said Louise as she handed paper towels to the girl.

'She's Jonno's wife.'

'And Jonno is…?'

'Skye's father.'

'I see.' Louise paused, careful not to let any reaction show on her face. 'So Jonno is married. Did you know that, Rosie?'

'Oh, yes, we all lived together on the site.' Carefully the girl dried her hands.

'So does Mitzi have children as well?' Louise knew she had to tread carefully.

'Yes,' Rosie said. 'Three. And the others,' she added. 'Amber has two children and Sharon had a baby last year.'

'And was Jonno the father of all these children?' asked Louise as she struggled to hide any emotion.

'Oh, yes.' Rosie nodded. 'It's like that on the site.' There was a note of defiance in her voice as if she dared Louise to challenge her explanation.

'So why did Mitzi come to see you?' By this time they had left the sluice and were approaching the ward. Through the glass partition Louise could see that Matt had returned to the ward while she had been away and, together with Nicky, was attending to Skye.

'She said they were moving on—to Glastonbury,' said Rosie. 'They went this morning,' she added sullenly. 'I told her I couldn't go with them, not yet. But I will, later. I'll get Skye sorted with someone, then I'll join them…' She fell silent as they approached Skye's incubator.

Matt and Nicky looked up. 'Hello, Rosie,' said Matt in his natural, friendly style, 'have you come to visit your daughter?'

Rosie stood alongside the incubator, staring down at Skye, her hands clenching and unclenching as for the first time she really looked at her baby. A variety of emotions flitted across her features—shock, horror even at the frailty of the baby before her. Then, even as Louise watched, there was something else, maybe simply a hint of curiosity—but it was a start.

'She's doing well,' Nicky began. 'She's a real little fighter.'

'What are all those tubes for?' demanded Rosie in a harsh whisper.

'Well,' said Matt, 'this one here is to help her to breathe, and this one, well, that is going into her tummy and it has two jobs—it's feeding her and it's also giving her any medication that she needs.'

'And those others on her chest—what are those for?' Rosie obviously hadn't finished.

'Those are connected up to this heart monitor,' Matt replied, indicating the machine behind him. 'It records Skye's heartbeat and will tell us immediately if there is any problem.'

'Isn't she cold? She's only got a nappy on.' Rosie frowned.

'No, she isn't cold,' Matt replied. 'A constant temperature is maintained inside the incubator—just as if she were still inside you. Look, why don't you see for yourself? You can touch her through this side panel here.' He slid back the panel as he spoke but Rosie drew back, and for a moment Louise thought Matt might have gone too far too soon. However, he chose to ignore Rosie's reaction, instead putting his own hand inside and gently touching the tiny baby, stroking first her arm, then her leg.

'I hope,' said Rosie after a moment of watching, 'that you've washed your hands.'

'I can assure you I have,' said Matt with a smile. 'We wouldn't put these precious little bundles under threat from infection. Now, Rosie, it's your turn.' Withdrawing his hand, he stood aside and at last Rosie stepped forward.

As happened so often in these situations, Louise found herself holding her breath, silently willing Rosie not to reject her baby, to reach out her hand and to touch her. And even as she watched, Rosie did just that. At first it was no more than a light touch with her index finger on the back of Skye's little hand. As the baby moved in an involuntarily movement, jerking both her arms and legs, Rosie recoiled, withdrawing her hand rapidly.

'It's all right, Rosie,' said Matt. 'She's just realised you're there, but she knows now and it's my guess she's delighted and is wanting you to touch her again.'

'D'you think so?' Rosie looked doubtful.

'Absolutely,' Matt replied firmly. 'She recognised her mum. She's probably been lying there for ages, just waiting for you to come. Go on, touch her again.'

Gingerly Rosie put her hand into the incubator again and this time, emboldened by Matt's words of encouragement, she first gently stroked Baby Skye's arm, and then her leg, just as Matt had done.

'She's opened her eyes,' she whispered at last.

'Why don't you sit beside her for a while?' suggested Louise, drawing up a chair.

'On my own?' Rosie looked up quickly, clearly terrified at such a prospect.

'I'll be nearby,' promised Nicky.

Rosie looked around the ward and it seemed that for the first time she realised there were other babies there, other babies just like Skye who had been born too early and who were all engaged in the same struggle. 'All right,' she said at last.

When Louise and Matt left the ward a few moments later Rosie was seated next to Skye's incubator, one hand through the aperture gently holding the baby's hand and with her gaze firmly fixed on her daughter's little scrunched-up face.

And later, much later, after Louise had supervised the airlift of baby William and was preparing to go off duty, Rosie came to the office.

'Hello, Rosie,' said Louise gently, noticing that the girl looked exhausted, her face pale and tear-stained. 'What is it? Are you ready to go back to your ward?'

Rosie shook her head and hovered in the doorway.

'What is it, then?'

'I want my mum,' she said, and by this time the tears were flowing freely down her cheeks.

'There's the phone,' said Louise. 'Why don't you give her a ring?'

Rosie nodded and, coming right into the office, sat down at the desk. She lifted the receiver and after several fumbling attempts dialled a number.

'Hello,' Louise heard her say at last. 'Mum? It's me, Rosie.'

CHAPTER NINE

'IT'S an appalling situation.' It was the following day and
Louise was in her office, discussing Rosie Bradley and
Skye with Michelle, social worker Judy Wingard and Matt.

'Let me get this straight,' said Judy. 'Are you saying
this guy Jonno was not only married with a family but had
children by other women as well as being father to Skye?'

'It seems that way,' Louise replied with a sigh, 'but the
really bizarre thing is that they all seem to live together.'

'A sort of commune, then?' Matt turned and looked
through the glass partition to where Rosie could be seen,
sitting beside Skye's incubator.

'Yes, and it was Jonno's wife Mitzi who came to see
Rosie to tell her they were moving on.'

'He was probably too much of a coward to come himself,' said Matt, his jaw tightening. 'I take it Rosie would
have been underage when she first went off with them?'

'Seems that way,' Louise agreed. 'She's still only sixteen now.'

'So what's the situation at the moment?' Judy turned to
look through the glass at Rosie. 'You say she phoned her
parents?'

Louise nodded. 'Yes, she spoke to her mother late
yesterday.'

'Whatever did she tell her?' asked Michelle.

'As far as I know, only that she was in Ellie's and had
had a baby. Her parents are coming in at eleven o'clock
this morning to see her.'

Instinctively they all turned to look at the clock.

'Ten to,' said Judy. 'I think, in that case, I'll go and make a couple more calls in the main hospital then I'll come back here a bit later. Maybe by then Rosie and her family might have had a chance to sort out what happens next. By the way, how is Skye this morning?' She was looking at Louise as she spoke but Louise turned to Matt.

'Dr Forrester?' she said. 'You've just examined Skye.'

Matt nodded. 'She's holding her own. She's a real little fighter and we have every reason to believe she'll pull through.'

'Well, let's hope so,' said Judy.

'She certainly deserves to after the start she's had,' said Michelle grimly as she left the office to let Judy out of the unit.

'I think,' said Louise, as she and Matt were left alone, 'I'll get Rosie into the relatives' room before her parents arrive.'

'Looks like you could be too late,' said Matt, craning his neck to look through the glass partition. 'Could that be them now?'

Louise turned sharply and saw that as Michelle had been showing Judy out of the unit she had also admitted a middle-aged couple.

'Oh, no,' she said, 'you're right. Well, never mind.' Catching Michelle's eye through the glass, she indicated for her to take them to the relatives' room. 'We'll do it the other way round, that's all.'

'Do you want me around?' asked Matt.

'Well...' Louise thought rapidly. 'I don't want to alarm them too much at this stage—after all, they've quite a lot to take in. I think perhaps if we allow them to have a bit of time with Rosie on their own, then after they've been told about Skye and the fact that she needs special care, perhaps you could come in, Matt, if you have the time. I'm sure they'll have questions they'll want to ask you.'

'Very well.' Matt nodded. 'In that case, in the meantime I think I'll go and have a chat with Tracey Barrett. She wants to talk to me about Oliver's progress and I see she has just come onto the ward.'

'I'll have a quick word with the Bradleys, then I'll come and fetch Rosie,' said Louise, following him out of the office.

Her first impression on entering the relatives' room was of a couple that had suffered more than their share of stress and anxiety in the recent past. Rosie's mother, with her pale blonde hair and blue eyes, was an older version of her daughter, but her face was etched with lines of worry and anguish while her husband looked grey and defeated.

'I'm Sister Keating,' said Louise, shutting the door behind her.

'Good morning, Sister.' The man stepped forward, 'Tom Bradley, and this is my wife, Jo.' They both shook hands with Louise.

'I'm also the manager in charge of the special care baby unit,' Louise went on. 'I believe your daughter Rosie rang you last evening.'

'Yes, she did.' Jo nodded. 'Can we see her?' she added anxiously.

'Of course you can,' Louise replied. 'I'll fetch her for you in a moment.'

'Is she all right, Sister?' asked Tom.

'She's doing very well,' Louise replied. 'What exactly did she tell you on the phone?' she asked, glancing at Rosie's mother.

'Just that she was safe and that...that she's had a baby. A little girl, she said.'

'That's right.' Louise smiled. 'A beautiful little girl.'

'Is there anything wrong with the baby?' asked Jo anxiously. 'You said this is a special care unit, didn't you?'

'Yes, it is,' Louise agreed.

'Isn't that where babies go when there's something wrong with them?'

'Not necessarily,' Louise replied, then briskly she added, 'But first things first. I'll go and fetch Rosie for you. You need to spend a bit of time catching up.' Leaving the Bradleys in the relatives' room, Louise made her way onto the ward.

Rosie was still sitting beside Skye's incubator, one hand through the aperture and with her head resting on the top.

'Rosie.' Gently Louise touched her shoulder and the girl jumped slightly, as if she had been dozing.

'What is it?' She looked up at Louise then immediately she turned her head and her gaze flew to her daughter. 'Is she all right?' she demanded.

'She's fine, Rosie. Your parents have just arrived.'

'What? Where?' Rosie looked round, an almost wild expression in her eyes.

'They are in the relatives' room,' Louise explained. 'Why don't you come through there with me now?'

'What about Skye?' Rosie stood up and looked down at her baby.

'We'll leave Skye where she is, then maybe a bit later on they can see her, if that's what you want, Rosie.'

Rosie nodded then followed Louise down the ward. As they passed Oliver Barrett's incubator Matt looked up from talking to Tracey and winked at Louise.

Louise knew it was because of the situation concerning Rosie but for a fraction of a second she felt ridiculously pleased, as if she and Matt were suddenly, unexpectedly sharing something again. She had no time to explore this intriguing possibility further for she and Rosie had almost reached the relatives' room.

'Is my dad there?' said Rosie warily.

'Yes, he is.' Louise nodded.

'How...how does he seem?'

'Just relieved that you're safe,' Louise replied.

'Not angry, then?' said Rosie.

'No, Rosie, not angry.' Louise opened the door, caught a glimpse of the expression on Jo Bradley's face—a mixture of apprehension and anxiety—preceded Rosie into the room, then stood aside.

For a long moment Rosie stood in the doorway, staring at her parents, then suddenly she quite literally threw herself across the room and into her mother's arms.

Quietly Louise withdrew from the room and closed the door.

'How did it go?' asked Matt a little later.

'They're still in there,' said Louise. 'But they've been quiet, no sounds of battle or anything.'

'I can't imagine how anyone would feel in those circumstances,' said Matt thoughtfully. 'Just imagine if your daughter had suddenly upped and left home, there'd been no word from her, then some considerable time later you get a call right out of the blue saying she's in hospital, having given birth to a baby...'

'I would think their first reaction was sheer relief at knowing that she was safe,' said Louise slowly. 'When you think about it, I doubt they've thought of much else since she left home. I gather from Rosie that she's their only child. Another thing you have to remember is that this is also their first grandchild we're talking about.'

'Did you tell them anything about Skye?' asked Matt. 'About how premature she was or anything like that?'

'No, not yet.' Louise shook her head, 'I thought it best

to get this first meeting over with. And while I take your point about how difficult it is for the Bradleys, you have to also see it from Rosie's point of view. This can't be easy for her either. She left home presumably because she'd met this Jonno character with whom she, no doubt, imagined herself to be in love, then found she was attracted by the hippy lifestyle of the travellers. When she became pregnant apparently Jonno wasn't too happy...'

'I bet he wasn't,' said Matt darkly, 'what with her being underage. On the other hand, from what we've heard, I couldn't imagine one more child would have made a lot of difference.'

'I think Rosie was of the impression that he would have accepted her baby in the end,' Louise replied thoughtfully. 'What, of course, she didn't bargain for was Skye being as premature as she was and needing special care. There was a point when I think she thought she could just move on and leave Skye here, but thankfully, over the last day or so, some bonding has taken place and I believe Rosie is now of the opinion that she can't leave Skye. At least I hope that's the case and that she isn't thinking that she can just leave her with her parents.'

'Do you think that might be what's going to happen?' Matt threw her a quick glance.

'I hope not,' said Louise. 'But I've been in this job long enough to know that anything can happen. I really felt last night that Rosie was desperately missing her own mum after finally facing up to the fact that she has become a mum herself. Let's just hope it all turns out to be for the right reasons.'

'Looks like we could be about to find out,' said Matt as the door to the relatives' room suddenly opened and Tom Bradley appeared.

'May we have a word?' he asked as he caught sight of Louise and Matt.

'Of course.' Indicating for Matt to join her, Louise followed Tom back into the relatives' room. From the appearance of Rosie and her mother, who were both red-eyed, it was obvious they had been crying while Tom, if it were possible, looked even greyer than he had on his arrival.

'This is Dr Matthew Forrester,' said Louise, turning as Matt closed the door behind him. 'He's registrar to our consultant paediatrician.'

'Rosie tells us that there are complications with the baby,' said Tom, coming straight to the point after shaking hands with Matt.

'Your granddaughter was born ten weeks prematurely,' explained Matt. 'She weighed only a little over two pounds so as you can imagine there are bound to be difficulties.'

'What sort of difficulties?' asked Jo anxiously.

'Well, her lungs weren't fully formed so she's having help with her breathing from a ventilator,' Matt explained. 'She also can't feed on her own,' he went on, 'so she's being fed intravenously. And because she was jaundiced at birth, she's also receiving photo therapy treatment.'

'Is she in any danger?' asked Tom.

'There's always an element of risk with these very tiny babies,' said Matt honestly, 'but at the same time, the survival rate for babies born at thirty weeks is high, so with the right specialist care, which she will receive here at Ellie's, there's every chance that she will progress normally.'

'How long will all this take?' asked Jo.

It was Louise who answered. 'We need to get Skye to a good weight—around five pounds—before we can consider her going home. That will probably take around the same time as if she had gone to full term.'

'So another ten weeks.' Jo glanced at her husband.

'Yes, about that,' replied Louise. 'Providing, of course, that there are no further complications, which could delay the time of discharge.'

'We've suggested that Rosie comes home with us,' began Tom.

'I'm not leaving Skye,' said Rosie bluntly, speaking for the first time since Louise and Matt had come into the room.

'But surely you won't be able to stay here at the hospital for all that time.' Jo Bradley threw Louise a quick look.

'No, unfortunately we don't have facilities for that,' Louise replied, 'although Rosie will be staying here until she's fully fit herself. After that she can visit Skye whenever she likes—every day if she wishes.'

'We live over fifty miles away,' said Tom. 'There's no way you could make that trip every day, Rosie,' he went on, turning to his daughter.

'Our social worker is coming to talk to you soon,' said Louise. 'Maybe she'll be able to come up with a solution.'

'What sort of solution?' asked Rosie suspiciously.

'I don't know for sure. Maybe you renting a room or a flat nearby, Rosie, just until Skye is strong enough to go home.'

'Is that really her name?' asked Tom. There was a touch of incredulity in his tone and Louise threw Rosie an anxious glance, remembering how it had been because she'd found her parents' attitudes and conventions so restrictive in the past that she'd left home in the first place.

'Yes,' said Rosie defiantly. 'There's nothing wrong with it. It's a lovely name.'

'And it certainly suits her,' said Matt, coming to the rescue.

'Would you like to come and see her now?' added Louise, following Matt's lead. 'What do you think, Rosie?' she added. 'Do you think Skye is ready to meet her grandparents?'

'Yeah, I guess.' Rosie lifted her chin.

Together they left the relatives' room and, accompanied by Matt, Louise led the way onto the ward and across to the incubator which was home to Skye. Only then did she step aside and allow Rosie to present her baby to her parents.

'There she is,' said Rosie, and there was no mistaking the pride in her voice as they all looked down at the little girl in the incubator clad only in a nappy, a cotton vest and a tiny pink hat.

There was a little gasp from Jo when she saw the size of her granddaughter but somehow she managed to change the usual comment when anyone saw a premature baby for the first time from 'Isn't she small?' to 'Isn't she beautiful?'

Louise caught Matt's eye and they both witnessed the relief on Rosie's face. 'Yes,' she agreed softly, 'she is, isn't she?'

For a moment Tom looked quite stricken, as if the temperature in the ward, the mass of equipment and monitors and the tubes that surrounded his tiny granddaughter were all too much for him. Matt, sensing his distress, came to the rescue once more by explaining the function of the various pieces of equipment around the incubator.

'You're quite right,' said Jo after a while, looking up at Matt. 'Skye is a lovely name and it really does suit her.'

They stayed round the incubator for only a short while then made their way back to the relatives' room to find that Gina had made them coffee and Judy Wingard had just arrived.

'I'll leave you to it,' murmured Matt. 'I need to get back to Paediatrics.'

'Thanks for staying,' said Louise. 'I do appreciate it.'

'All part of the service,' said Matt with a grin. 'I hope they can work things out from here on.'

'I'm sure they will,' Louise replied, and then, as he would have gone, she said, 'Oh, Matt?'

'Yes?' He paused and looked back.

'Don't forget the rehearsal tomorrow night.'

'As if I could.' He pulled a face.

'Are you all ready for Saturday?' she asked, knowing he had a tendency to leave things until the very last minute, always believing he had plenty of time and not allowing for the possibility that something could go wrong. 'Have you got everything you need?'

'I think so.' He nodded. 'Only the hire suit to come now and I'm all set. I've bought a new shirt,' he added. 'Thought I'd better, especially as you seem to use mine for doing decorating and gardening.'

'It was only the one,' she protested. 'And that was one you no longer wore.'

With a grin and a wave of his hand he was gone, and a little later Jo and Tom Bradley also took their leave, promising to return the following day.

'There,' said Louise to Rosie as the doors shut behind them, 'that wasn't so bad, was it?'

Rosie shook her head. 'No,' she said, 'it wasn't as bad as I thought it would be. I thought they would be angry, especially my dad.'

'They are just relieved to know you are safe. You are their daughter, Rosie, their only daughter, and I think now you know how you would feel if you thought Skye was in danger.'

'Yes, I guess I do. I wish…' She paused. 'I wish now I hadn't put them through it, but at the time all I could think about was Jonno and how much I loved him. I knew there was no way they would have let me be with him, so in the end the only way was to just go…'

'But really they would have been right, wouldn't they, Rosie, not to let you go with Jonno?' said Louise quietly.

'Yeah, I s'ppose.' Rosie looked at the floor. 'But he isn't a bad person,' she said after a moment, 'just different, that's all.'

'Did you know he was married—at the beginning I mean—when you first met him?'

'No.' Rosie shook her head. 'I met him in the precinct—he seemed to always be there on Saturday mornings when I went shopping. He started buying me a drink, then one day he took me to the site where he lived. There were lots of other people there, and they were all very kind to me. I met Mitzi but no one said she was Jonno's wife. Anyway, I started going there regularly—I told my mum and dad I was at my friend's house and they believed me. After a time Jonno said they were moving on to a site near Stonehenge and he…Jonno said I could go with them.'

'Were you in love with Jonno by this time, Rosie?' asked Louise gently.

'Oh, yes,' said Rosie, and when she looked up there were tears in her eyes.

'And how old were you then?'

'I was fifteen,' she replied. 'That's why Jonno wasn't happy when I got pregnant.'

'I see,' said Louise quietly.

'If I had gone to full term I would have gone on to

Glastonbury with Jonno and the others...' Her eyes suddenly filled with tears.

'But is that the life you would have wanted for your daughter?' asked Louise.

'I don't know.' Rosie shook her head and looked at the floor again, then in an attempt to defend her friends, she said, 'it was a wonderful life in some ways. It was so free...so... Oh, I don't know...' The tears trickled down her cheeks and she dashed them away with the back of her hand.

'The trouble is,' she went on after a moment, 'I think I'm going to find it very hard, going back to my old way of life...'

'Yes, Rosie, I'm sure you will,' said Louise, 'but don't you think you owe it to Skye to give her the best life possible, especially after the rocky start she's had?'

'Yeah, I s'ppose.' Rosie nodded and kicked at the edge of the carpet with the toe of one of her boots.

'Well, enough of that now.' Louise stood up, 'I think it's time you got back to Maternity for lunch then a rest.'

After Rosie had gone Louise went back on the ward to do her midday check. She found Nicky changing Skye's nappy.

'How did it go with the grandparents?' asked Nicky curiously.

'Pretty well really, given the circumstances.' Louise looked down at the tiny girl who unknowingly had become the centre of so much attention.

'What do you think will happen now?'

'Well, hopefully Rosie, with the help of her parents, will find local accommodation until Skye is ready to leave us, then they'll both return to her parents' home in Reading.'

'And the infamous Jonno?'

'With any luck he'll never contact Rosie again,' said

Louise grimly. 'Somehow I doubt he will because Rosie was underage when she first went with him, and he must know that we're now aware of that. But if he does, I fear that Rosie may not have the strength to resist him or his bizarre way of life.'

The rehearsal for Michelle's and Andy's wedding took place in church on the Wednesday before the actual ceremony. Together with the bride and groom and Louise and Matt, Peter Colbert, the vicar of the parish church of Franchester, put Michelle's father, the two small attendants and the ushers through their paces. Afterwards some of the party found themselves in Angelo's.

'I'm sure I'll never get it right.' Andy looked quite pale. 'There's a lot more to say than I thought.'

'But we went through it all before,' said Michelle. 'We read through it with the vicar when we went to see him and then we went through it again on our own.'

'I know,' said Andy miserably, 'but it didn't seem so much then. Reading it is one thing, saying it aloud is something else, and saying it aloud in front of a church full of people is a whole new ball game.'

'You'll be all right,' said Matt cheerfully.

'It's all right for you,' said Andy. 'If I remember rightly, you didn't have half as much to say when you got married and you only had a couple of us there watching you.'

'I know,' Matt replied, and Louise found herself wondering if she was the only one who had caught the note of regret in his voice.

Later, when she was alone once more in the little house they had once shared, she found herself wondering if it would have been any different if she and Matt had done things differently.

Just suppose she hadn't got pregnant when she had, that

they had both completed their training then Matt had asked her to marry him. Suppose she had accepted and they had planned their wedding in as much meticulous detail as Michelle and Andy had theirs. Would things have turned out differently or would their marriage still have ended in the same way?

Presumably if they had done things in the conventional way they would have married at her parents' home in Dorset with a service at St Mary's, the parish church, followed by a reception at The George—the best hotel in the village. Michelle would have been her attendant and maybe Andy would have been Matt's best man. Her father would have been proud to give her away but at the same time she knew he would have been choked and her mother would have flapped and fussed just like Michelle's mother was doing.

But she had saved them all that, she told herself firmly, to say nothing of all the expense. At the time she had almost convinced herself that they were probably grateful to her if the truth be known, even though that hadn't been the impression she'd been given when she and Matt had travelled down to Dorset to see them to tell them that not only had she and Matt married but they, her parents, were shortly to become grandparents.

Her mother had cried, as Louise had suspected she might, and her father had huffed and puffed a bit, even though at one point his eyes also had been suspiciously bright. When they had left, she had come away with the uneasy feeling that, actually, her parents would have preferred all the fuss and the expense to the way things had turned out.

She and Matt had invited her parents to stay several times in the early stages of her pregnancy and it had been almost as if all four of them had been trying to compensate for what they had missed. And it had been during this time that her parents had grown very fond of Matt.

So, would it have been different? She may well have gone on to become pregnant in time, may even have lost that first baby, but would she and Matt have gone on to separate, to be where they were now, on the very edge of divorce?

Quite suddenly Louise found herself doubting it, because if it had all happened in the way she was imagining then it would have been because Matt had wanted to marry her in the first place, because she had wanted to marry him, because the time had been right for them both and because they hadn't felt under any pressure to do so. Instead, the way she felt now was that it had all been a dreadful mistake.

Sometimes, inevitably, she had also wondered what would have happened if her baby had lived, but that was an avenue she still found extremely painful and difficult to explore. Maybe everything would have been all right—who knew? Or equally, maybe they would still have found themselves in the same situation they were today.

All Louise really knew was that she was beginning to find the whole thing an incredible strain, having Matt so close, and that she would be relieved when the weekend, and Michelle's and Andy's wedding, was over.

CHAPTER TEN

FROM very early on Saturday morning the sun struggled to penetrate the mist, which hung over the river and drifted wraith-like through the willows and across the distant water meadows. Louise was up early and had showered and dressed and was enjoying orange juice and toast on the balcony when her phone rang.

'Just thought I'd make sure you were up,' said Matt, and for some reason at the sound of his voice her heart turned over. 'Can't have the chief attendant being late. I understand that's the prerogative of the bride.'

'The bride won't be late either, not if I've got anything to do with it,' said Louise lightly. 'And while we're on that subject, shouldn't you be checking on the groom?'

'I've already done that,' said Matt. 'He's cut himself shaving apparently but apart from that I think he's on course—I'm on my way over to his flat now.'

'And I'll soon be going to help Michelle.'

'Looks like it's going to be a fine day.'

'Yes, looks that way,' she agreed.

'Right.' It was obvious he wasn't sure what else to say. 'I'll see you in church then.'

'Yes, all right, Matt, see you in church,' she agreed faintly. She replaced the receiver and for a long moment sat staring at the phone, her mind in turmoil. Then, taking a deep breath, she stood up and went to get ready.

Michelle's parents, Sue and Henry Burns, lived in a beautiful house on the far side of Franchester set back from the road amidst a mass of mimosa and flowering cherry trees. A marquee had been erected on the lawns at the rear of the house to accommodate the many guests who had travelled from far and wide for the wedding of the couple's only daughter to Andy Steane.

When Louise arrived, parking her car carefully in a corner of the drive well away from the main area that would later be filled with guests' cars, the house was already humming with an air of excitement. A caterers' van was parked in front of the main entrance and trays of food were being carried into the house, while from another smaller van two women were transporting large floral arrangements, bouquets, posies and dozens of buttonholes.

Sue was in the spacious hallway of the house, apparently directing traffic. 'That's right,' she was saying as Louise came through the door, 'flowers through there, those trays straight into the marquee and—' She broke off as she saw Louise. 'Oh, Louise, good, there you are. Go straight up. Michelle is in her old room—the hairdresser and the manicurist will be here at any moment.'

Louise opened her mouth to speak but, realising instantly that she had lost Sue's attention, closed it again and scurried up the stairs to Michelle's bedroom. She found her friend in her bathrobe, pale-faced but calm, sitting on her bed surrounded by tissue paper, lace and satin lingerie and talking on her mobile phone.

Michelle waved to Louise then said into the phone, 'So, he's just arrived? That's good. I can leave you in capable hands, then?' She smiled. 'Yes, Lou is here, too. Just keep telling yourself…' she glanced at her bedside clock '…in five hours or so it'll all be over and you'll be able to relax and enjoy yourself…. Yes, I know you'll still have your speech to do, but you'll be fine, Andy, you really will. No, we can't just forget it all and go straight off on honeymoon. What? Yes, darling, I love you, too. I'll see you in church.'

With a sigh she disconnected and looked at Louise. 'I'm beginning to wonder if it was fair to put Andy through all this,' she said. 'He's as nervous as a rabbit this morning. Thank goodness he's got Matt with him. I think if it had been his brother he wouldn't have been any better than Andy, but if anyone can get him into shape and through this it will be Matt.'

The next couple of hours passed in a whirl of hairdressing, manicuring and make-up, followed by the arrival of four-year-old Mollie, who was to be Michelle's flower girl, and her pageboy, Jack, who proudly told everyone that he was nearly five. Mrs Nesbitt was on hand to administer any last-minute adjustments to Michelle's dress and at last, after helping Michelle, it was time for Louise to step into her own dress.

It felt good as the creamy folds of satin settled softly against her hips then swirled round her ankles. This was how her own wedding day should have been, she thought with a pang of regret, but it was no good thinking about that now, her own day, vastly different had gone and this was Michelle's day.

When they were ready they left the bedroom and went down to the drawing room where Henry Burns, distinguished-looking in his morning suit, appeared to go into shock at the sight of his daughter in her wedding dress and Sue, resplendent in oyster dress and coat, was forced to dab at her eyes beneath the wide brim of her hat.

'Don't, Mum, please,' said Michelle warningly, 'you'll start me off.'

'I know. I'm sorry,' said Sue with a sniff. 'It's just that you look so beautiful…doesn't she, Henry?'

'Just like a princess,' her husband agreed with a catch

in his voice, and briefly Louise found herself thinking of her own parents and of how they would have loved seeing her like this.

'I'm a pwincess, too,' said Mollie, her little face earnest.

'Yes, darling,' said Michelle as everyone laughed, relieved that the emotion of the moment had been diffused, 'you're a princess, too.'

Photographs followed as the official photographer, an amiable little man with wild, black curls and dark-rimmed glasses, cajoled and bullied them into the poses he wanted—Michelle, carrying her bouquet of lilies and cream roses, on the staircase, in the garden, with her mother, with Louise and the children and, finally, with her father.

At last they were ready to leave for the church. Sue and Michelle were with Mollie and Jack in a silver Rolls Royce, leaving Michelle to follow with her father in a vintage, dark green Bentley.

It was only a short distance to the church and by the time they left the house every tendril of the early morning mist had disappeared, giving way to a glorious late spring day of blue skies, blossom and bright sunshine. As they drew up outside the church the photographer hurried forward for more shots.

'That's the same man who was at your house,' said Jack in awe, turning to Michelle's mother.

'Yes, it is,' Sue agreed, 'and I think, Jack, you'll be seeing quite a lot of him today.'

There was a short wait in the church porch while from inside drifted the strains of Bach. Michelle arrived with her father, and after adjustments to her dress and more photographs they formed themselves into the bridal procession, the notes from the organ swelled, Bach gave way to 'The Bridal March' and with Louise walking behind

Michelle and Henry, and behind her, Jack, and Mollie with her basket of rose petals, the long walk to the altar began.

Louise's first impression as they came into the church out of the bright sunlight and turned into the central aisle was of a sea of hats, hats of every size and every colour. And the flowers, floral set pieces and posies on the ends of the pews in the white and cream of Michelle's bouquet and whose fragrance, mingling with that of incense and beeswax, filled the air. She was aware of the hats moving, of heads turning, of people craning their necks to see Michelle. There were fleeting glimpses of familiar faces, of mutual friends and colleagues. She saw the smiles of approval, handkerchiefs held to damp eyes, shafts of sunlight that pierced the jewel-like brilliance of stained-glass windows, and was aware of Michelle's dress and the folds of her train dragging slightly, pulled by the pile of the red and blue carpet as she moved slowly and proudly to meet her bridegroom.

Then they were there, and Andy and Matt, achingly handsome in morning suits, were turning to greet Michelle. The vicar, resplendent in ceremonial cope moved forward to greet them and momentarily Louise was aware of the expression on Matt's face as his gaze turned from Michelle and came to rest on her.

In that moment it was as if this was their wedding day all over again and he was turning to welcome her. Wonderingly, his gaze took in her dress with its beaded bodice and softly flowing skirt, her hair with its diamanté clip, the cream and shell pink roses she carried, finally coming back to her eyes, holding her gaze as if searching to find his own emotions reflected there, before turning at last to witness what was taking place before him.

And Louise herself was suddenly filled with a feeling of such peace and happiness it was almost beyond description as the vicar opened the ceremony in the time-honoured way. 'Dearly beloved, we are gathered here to-day in the sight of God and in the face of this congregation to witness the joining together of this man and this woman in holy matrimony...'

Michelle and Andy had decided on the traditional service from the Book of Common Prayer, together with old and much-loved hymns, prayers and the reading from Corinthians about love. The strains of 'Love Divine' filled the church followed by the beautiful and poignant words of the marriage vows... 'To have and to hold...from this day forward...in sickness and in health...until death us do part...' And throughout it all, for Louise, standing there behind Michelle as she made those solemn vows to Andy, it was as if it was a reminder to her, and to Matt, of the commitment they had once made to each other, and she found herself having to fight the lump that had risen in her throat as she tried not to dwell on the fact that they were about to break that commitment.

During the signing of the register the choir sang Schubert's 'Ave Maria' and almost before Louise knew it the strains of 'The Wedding March' rose to the rafters and Matt was taking her arm for the triumphant procession down the aisle behind Michelle and Andy and their parents, and the happiness she had felt throughout the service seemed to flow through her very veins and explode, together with the tumultuous peal of bells, as they stepped out of the church into the warmth of the spring sunshine.

The little photographer darted here, there and everywhere, flash bulbs popped, confetti filled the air, kisses were exchanged and hats admired.

'Doesn't she look lovely?' Suddenly Nicky was at Louise's side. 'That dress is exquisite.'

'She looks radiant,' Louise replied, 'quite radiant.'

And she did. If happiness could be summed up in one word that day it would have been Michelle—Michelle as she gazed into Andy's eyes as they posed for photographs, Michelle as she accepted compliments and congratulations from family and friends, and Michelle as she had exchanged her lifelong vows with the man she loved.

Champagne was awaiting the wedding party and their guests on their return to the house and after yet more photographs they all made their way into the marquee where the guests took their places at round tables covered with cream damask cloths and bearing centrepieces of pink and cream roses. Louise found herself seated beside Matt at the long table reserved for the wedding party.

'Shouldn't I be on the other side, near Michelle?' she whispered to Matt.

'I swapped the name cards,' he murmured.

'Why?' Her eyes widened.

'Because I wanted to sit next to you. Surely no one can object to that...'

'I wouldn't be too sure about that,' Louise replied wryly. 'Michelle's mum is giving you some very frosty looks. Michelle told me she spent weeks on the seating plan.'

'Leave Michelle's mum to me.' Standing up, Matt moved swiftly down the table and took Sue's hand in his. When she looked up, he gazed down into her eyes, then bent his head and whispered something into her ear. He was back with only seconds to spare before the vicar brought the guests to their feet while he said grace.

'Whatever did you say to her?' whispered Louise as they sat down again. 'She's positively beaming at us. I thought she'd be furious with anyone who messed up her arrangements.'

'I'll tell you later,' he replied smoothly, then, before she could protest, he added, 'You look wonderful, you know, Louise, in that dress.'

'Thank you.' She smiled.

'I mean it. I know it's Michelle's day and she looks lovely, too, but there's something about you in that dress...' He trailed off, shaking his head as if unable to continue. He was saved by the arrival of the food—cream of asparagus soup, followed later by Scottish salmon then noisettes of lamb marinated in rosemary sauce and served with tender baby vegetables. For dessert there were individual pavlovas filled with raspberries and kiwi-fruit and each course was accompanied by the finest wines.

After coffee the bride and groom were called upon to cut the three-tier cake, which was decorated with tiny replicas of Michelle's bouquet, and while the caterers whipped the cake away to be cut into portions, champagne was poured and Henry rose to his feet for his speech. It was inevitably an emotional speech, ending in sympathetic applause before Henry proposed a toast. 'Michelle and Andy, the bride and groom.'

'Michelle and Andy!'

'The bride and groom!' The company rose to its feet, raising their glasses, and then it was Andy's turn. His nervousness was almost tangible as in the time-honoured fashion he began, 'On behalf of my lovely wife and myself...' He went on to thank all those who needed to be thanked. He ended his speech by thanking the attendants and inviting everyone to raise their glasses and to drink a toast to Louise, and to Mollie and Jack.

As he sank down onto his chair in obvious relief, Matt rose to his feet to reply. Looking up at him, Louise was suddenly and unexpectedly overwhelmed by a sudden flood of emotion at the sight of the handsome man at her side. There was no trace of nerves as he captured his audience, held them by recounting a few amusing incidents from the student life he and Andy had shared then went on to produce roars of laughter with a couple of further well-chosen anecdotes. He ended by reading a few of the many messages of goodwill the couple had received from friends living abroad who had been unable to attend the ceremony.

The celebrations continued into the evening with the marquee being cleared for dancing and the jazz band that had been playing throughout the afternoon being replaced by a disco.

Michelle and Andy were invited to lead the dancing to the strains of 'Unchained Melody', which Louise knew had always been 'their song'.

'Shall we join them?' murmured Matt in her ear as Sue and Henry and Andy's parents took to the floor. And it seemed the most natural thing to do as she slipped easily into his arms and they danced to the familiar strains of the song beloved by lovers everywhere.

'Are you happy?' he murmured once against her cheek.

'Oh, yes,' she replied dreamily, 'very.'

'Me, too,' he sighed, and held her even closer.

And she was, Louise thought, almost in surprise. At that moment, dancing with Matt at her best friend's wedding, she was at peace with herself and with the world. No matter that soon, after this day was over, they had agreed to set in motion the chain of events that would bring their own marriage to an end, able for the time being to forget that and to enjoy the simple pleasure of being in his arms again.

And it was a pleasure, she realised with a sudden little sense of shock. It had been a pleasure when they had danced before at the club, however briefly, and when Matt had kissed her, although she had put that down to the

drink. And maybe that's all this was, she told herself ruefully, because when all was said and done the champagne
had flowed freely that day. But, whatever it was, it still
felt good and she was aware of admiring glances from their
friends and colleagues and from Angelo and Maria, who
had closed the restaurant that day to attend the wedding,
as if they all wholly approved of what they were seeing.

All too soon the number was over, but far from releasing
her, Matt continued to hold her throughout the following
two numbers and only let her go after extracting a promise
that she would dance again with him later.

'Of course,' she agreed with a laugh. 'But you must
dance with other women.'

'Who do you mean?' he asked warily.

'Well, Michelle...'

'Of course.'

'And her mum.'

'Really?'

'Yes, and Andy's mum and—'

'All right, I get the picture.' He sighed. 'I'll continue
with my duties as best man until the very end.'

Louise smiled as he moved away and she saw him dancing with other women, but later, as she danced with an
uncle of Michelle's, she caught sight of Tina Gordon in
Matt's arms, smiling up at him and whispering in his ear,
and she felt a profound stab of something so painful she
could only believe it to be jealousy. Which was crazy really when she considered just where they were in their
marriage and where it was going. She knew in the future
she was simply going to have to get used to seeing other
women with Matt because there was no way that a man
like him was going to be on his own for long. Already
Tina had expressed interest in Matt and at the same time
had indicated a willingness on his part, so it wasn't really

surprising they had sought each other out to dance, she thought miserably as Michelle's uncle twirled her round a few times at the end of the number.

The dancing continued well into the evening until Louise slipped away with Michelle into the house to help her with her overnight bag in preparation for the short journey to the hotel where she and Andy were to spend their wedding night before leaving for the Caribbean the following day.

'It's been the most wonderful day of my life,' sighed Michelle as Louise slipped a satin wrap around her shoulders.

'Just go on being happy,' whispered Louise as Michelle turned to face her.

'Oh, I will, I will.' Wordlessly the two friends hugged, the impending situation between Louise and Matt remaining an unspoken issue between them but Michelle obviously only too aware that by the time she returned from honeymoon the countdown to her friends' divorce could be well under way.

Moments later they descended the stairs to find Andy waiting for them and the vintage Bentley at the door once more as tearful farewells followed from parents and close family. The word had gone round that the bride and groom were about to leave for people, festooned with streamers, poured out of the marquee, some clutching helium-filled balloons and others running forward to shower Andy and Michelle with handfuls of confetti as they climbed into the back of the car.

Some enthusiastic person had tied a large black boot and half a dozen cans to the bumper of the car, and as the driver drew away amidst a flurry of goodbyes and shrieks of laughter, a sudden shower of rockets soared into the night sky from the back of the house and burst into an explosion of brightly coloured stars, bringing forth cries of surprise and delight from the onlookers.

And quite suddenly, as Louise watched and waved, Matt was there beside her with one arm around her shoulders, and in that moment she knew she was content for it to be that way and that she didn't have the slightest inclination to push him away.

'Well,' Matt said, as the car finally disappeared out of the drive and onto the main road and people began to turn away, 'that's that. Do you think that's the end of our duties now or are we expected to help with the clearing-up?'

Louise shook her head. 'No,' she said, 'I asked Sue that just now and she said we've more than done our bit in looking after Michelle and Andy all day and that the caterers have been employed to clear everything up. She said the disco is going on for at least another hour and that we should enjoy ourselves.'

Matt didn't answer and she looked up at him. 'Matt?' she said.

'I was wondering,' he said. 'Do you think we would be missed if we didn't go back?'

'I shouldn't think so,' she replied. 'I would imagine by now that those who are left wouldn't have much idea of who else was there.'

'That's what I thought,' he said.

'Why?' she asked curiously when he didn't elaborate any further.

'I thought perhaps we also could slip away,' he said softly at last.

'Like Michelle and Andy, you mean?'

'Well, perhaps not with quite so much ballyhoo, just quietly without anyone noticing, so to speak.'

'I'm sure we could. It has been quite a day—it would be rather nice to relax for a bit.'

'That's exactly what I was thinking.'

'What did you have in mind?' She threw him a curious glance, aware at the same time of a sudden tingle of excitement.

'I thought I might take you home.'

'Not after all that champagne,' she protested. 'We'll have to leave our cars here.'

'I didn't mean by car,' he replied lightly. 'I thought perhaps I'd walk you home. But on the other hand, if you're too tired, I could call a cab.'

'No,' she said reflectively, 'a walk sounds rather nice. We'll probably get some funny looks—you in your morning suit and me in this dress—but who cares?'

'My sentiments exactly,' he replied. 'Who cares?'

Somehow, they managed to slip away without anyone noticing and together they ran hand in hand down the drive to the road, leaving the lighted house behind them and the sounds of revelry pouring out of the marquee.

It was a soft spring night and beneath a wide starlit sky they strolled through the quiet, almost deserted streets of Franchester, Louise with Matt's jacket around her shoulders over her exquisite satin beaded dress and with coloured streamers and confetti in her hair, and Matt in his pinstriped trousers, minus his cravat, with the top buttons of his shirt undone and a bottle of champagne in one hand.

A roving police car pulled up alongside them at one point, one of the two officers inside lowering his window. 'Is everything all right, sir?' he asked Matt.

'Yes, Officer,' Matt replied. 'Everything is wonderful.'

'In that case, I'll bid you both goodnight,' said the policeman with a grin.

'So you've enjoyed yourself?' asked Louise, throwing Matt a sidelong glance as the police car pulled away from the kerb and went on its way into the night.

'Oh, yes,' Matt replied. 'I've had a marvellous time. Haven't you?' He looked down at her.

'Yes.' She smiled. 'It's been great.' In silence they walked past Angelo's, in darkness tonight, its shutters closed, and then they reached the front door of the middle house of the terrace, the one that was painted pink.

Louise wasn't quite sure what would happen next, but at the same time, somehow, she had a pretty good idea because throughout the day, from the very moment that Matt had turned from the altar and caught sight of her, the tension had been growing between them, building steadily towards this very moment.

With hands that were shaking slightly she inserted her key in the lock. 'Will you...will you come in?' she asked, trying to keep her voice as light as possible.

'Why not?' he said with a little sigh. 'After all, it would be a pity to waste this champagne.'

CHAPTER ELEVEN

'I'M NOT SURE that should have happened,' said Louise, stretching luxuriously.

'Why not?' Propping himself on one elbow, Matt looked down at her where she lay against the pillows of the large double bed they had once shared and which she hadn't slept in since he had left. 'We are still married after all.'

'I know, but the way I understand it, we have to convince a judge that our marriage has irretrievably broken down—I'm not sure what we just did constitutes that.'

'It was good, though, wasn't it?' He grinned at her and began winding a strand of her hair round his finger.

'Yes, Matt,' she admitted, knowing because he knew her so well that to lie or to argue would be pointless, 'it was good.'

'But, then, it always was,' he said lightly. 'There never was any problem with that.'

It was true, she thought as briefly she closed her eyes, sex always had been wonderful. At least, it had been to start with, until things between them had become impossible. And it had been good last night following the wonderful day they had shared. It was early morning now and beyond the window she could hear the birds singing and the intermittent call of the ducks on the river below.

At the foot of the bed her dress was draped over a chair placed there the night before by Matt who had then gone on to slowly remove first her stockings, then unfasten one by one the hooks of the camisole she had worn under her dress. His own clothes were strewn around the room, hurriedly discarded as their need for each other had finally overwhelmed them both.

Their lovemaking had been tumultuous, with a kind of desperation about it but at the same time with a feeling of inevitability, almost of coming home, which had left Louise thoroughly confused. Here they were on the very brink of divorce yet able to still enjoy such wonderful sex—it made no sense, no sense at all. Opening her eyes, she stole a glance at Matt and was disconcerted to see a look of amusement on his face.

'What are you laughing at?' she said indignantly.

'I wasn't laughing, not really, I was just thinking about Michelle's mum when she realised her seating plan had been messed up.'

'So, what did you say to her?' asked Louise curiously.

'You mean after I'd told her she could be mistaken for Michelle's sister?' He grinned. 'Well, I confessed to having done it,' he admitted, 'then I told her that I was certain she wouldn't want to be held responsible for keeping a man apart from his wife. She didn't really have any choice after that.'

'That's OK,' said Louise slowly, 'but presumably Michelle would have told her we're about to divorce. She probably now thinks she's responsible for bringing about a reconciliation.'

'Well, if it makes her happy to think that,' said Matt with a shrug.

For a moment Louise thought he was going to say that maybe they shouldn't disappoint her, but he didn't.

'I have to get up,' she said after a while.

'Do you? Why?' It was Matt's turn to sound disappointed.

'I have things to do.'

He sighed. 'Yes, I guess I do as well. But...five more

minutes wouldn't hurt...' As he spoke his arm crept around her waist.

'No, Matt,' she said firmly, 'I'm going to run a bath.' Slipping out of bed and into a robe, Louise was suddenly aware of her nakedness and hurried to the bathroom, knowing full well what would happen if she stayed and not knowing quite how much more her emotions could cope with.

Turning the bath taps on full, she added a generous amount of scented bath oil and when the bath was half-full and steam was filling the bathroom she discarded her robe and stepped into the foaming water. With a sigh she slid down into the bubbles and, leaning her head back, relaxed and closed her eyes.

If she was honest, the previous day had been one of the happiest of her life, and in spite of the fact that it had been Michelle's and Andy's day, because Matt had been at her side throughout it all it had almost been as if they had been reliving their own wedding day but at the same time adding to it all the bits they had missed out on—the church ceremony, the music, the flowers, the reception and the dancing. Not, of course, that all those things, if they had done them, would have made the slightest difference to the way things had turned out between them...but it did no harm to fantasize...

'Penny for them?'

Louise's eyes snapped open. Matt, clad only in a pair of briefs, had come into the bathroom and was casually perched on the side of the bath, in just the way he'd done when they'd first been married. 'What do you mean?' she frowned.

'Your thoughts,' he said in the same light tone. 'You appeared to be daydreaming.'

'Yes, I was,' she said slowly.

'So, are you going to tell me? Come on,' he said, picking up a sponge, 'lean forward and I'll wash your back.'

'I was thinking about yesterday,' she said as she found herself obeying him, leaning forward then responding to the firm touch of his hands as he soaped her back.

'What about yesterday?'

'About how wonderful it all was...and yet how different it was to...to our day...' There, she'd said it now, and as she did so the sureness of Matt's touch faltered for a fraction of a second. It would have been imperceptible to anyone but Louise, who was his wife, who knew what his reaction would be and who knew he wouldn't have expected her to say that.

'Yes,' he agreed softly, 'it was different but the intentions and the sentiments surely were the same.'

'Yes, I guess.' She raised her shoulders. 'Let's just hope they have more luck than we did.'

'You think it's all down to luck?' he said quietly.

'No, of course not, not all of it, but to whatever that magic ingredient it is that makes it a success,' she said, shuddering with delight as he squeezed warm water over her back and shoulders. And still he didn't go, staying there while she finished her bath then holding a towel for her when she stepped out, enfolding her in its fluffy depths as if it was the most natural thing in the world that he should be there to do so.

He continued to hold her close for a while until at last with a sigh he released her.

'I'll have a shower,' he said almost reluctantly, as if some spell had been re-created between them in the last twenty-four hours and he didn't want to be the one to break it.

'And I'll go and fix us some breakfast,' she replied faintly, knowing that if they stayed there like that, with her enfolded in his arms, for a moment longer she would have given in and they would have gone straight back to bed.

Matt left after breakfast, going back to his rooms at the hospital to pack up his hire suit and then to keep a pre-arranged lunch date with Neil Richardson and his wife Izzy.

'I don't really want to go,' he'd said as he'd helped himself to more toast liberally spreading it with marmalade, 'but I think they feel sorry for me. Being on my own and all that. What will you do today?' he'd added, looking up, the toast poised halfway to his mouth.

'Oh, don't worry about me,' she'd replied, 'I've got loads to do, absolutely loads.'

'Oh, well, that's all right, then,' he'd said with a little shrug.

The trouble was, it wasn't true. Louise didn't really have very much to do at all and if she was honest, after the excitement of the previous day—and night—the day ahead threatened to be something of an anticlimax. And after Matt had gone and she was alone she was reluctantly forced to admit that, really, she would have liked nothing better than for them to spend the day together.

'That is wonderful, Pauline. Look, Beth has put on four ounces.' It was three days after the wedding and Louise had just come onto the ward to watch while the babies were being weighed. It was always a tense moment for any parents who were present while they waited to see whether their son or daughter had made progress since the last time they had been weighed.

'So what does that make her now?' Eagerly Pauline leaned forward.

'She's just a fraction under four pounds,' replied Nicky, as she gently supported Beth in the sling they used to weigh the babies.

'That's good,' said Pauline slowly, 'but there's still a way to go before she reaches five pounds.'

'But just think how far she's come,' said Louise. 'She was a little scrap of a thing when she first came to us.'

'I know,' said Pauline, her eyes misting over at the memory. 'Malcolm still can't get over how tiny she was—he says her little feet were no bigger than the feet on our Lucy's dolls.'

'Louise, have you got a minute?' Louise looked up and saw that Roma had come into the ward.

'Yes, Roma, what is it?' she said.

'Mike Collard is in your office. He'd like a word with you.'

'Thanks, Roma, I'll come and see him now. Do you know what it's about?'

'No.' Roma shook her head. 'But I've put the kettle on—he'll be wanting his cup of tea.'

'Good thinking, Roma,' said Louise with a chuckle.

She found the chaplain in her office, looking out of the window at the mass of narcissi and deep purple polyanthus in the flower-beds outside.

'Mike, hello,' she said, coming right into the room and shutting the door behind her.

'Hello, Louise.' He turned sharply. 'I was just admiring the flowers.'

'There're lovely, aren't they? They've been particularly good this year,' she agreed. 'How are you, Mike?'

'Not so bad,' he said. 'A few aches and pains, but I mustn't grumble. There are a lot who are worse off than me.'

'You wanted to see me, I believe,' said Louise. 'Roma's put the kettle on for tea.'

'That sounds the best idea I've heard all day.' Mike's blue eyes twinkled. 'I've had a call, Louise,' he went on, growing serious again, 'from a couple whose baby was on this unit two years ago.'

'Before my time, then,' said Louise with a frown.

'Yes, it would be,' Mike agreed. 'Unfortunately their little one was one of those who didn't make it. I'm told he was just too small and he died when he was only two days old. Anyway, today is the anniversary of that day and his parents rang me to ask if they could come into the unit to view the book of remembrance.'

'Of course they can,' said Louise. 'Did they say what time?'

'Well, I said I would check with you first. They suggested one-thirty, and they also want me to come along and say a prayer with them.'

'One-thirty will be absolutely fine,' said Louise, glancing up as Roma suddenly tapped on the door and entered the room, bearing a tray of tea.

A little later, as Louise was showing Mike out of the unit, she met Rosie, who was coming in.

'They said I could go today,' said Rosie warily.

'Well, that's marvellous,' replied Louise.

'I don't want to leave Skye,' muttered Rosie, as she followed Louise to the sluice. She needed no reminders to scrub her hands these days before entering the ward.

'I know,' said Louise gently. 'Where will you be going?'

'Mum has found a flat and she says she's going to stay there with me until Skye is ready to leave hospital. Dad will have to go home because of his job but he'll come over at weekends.'

'Well, I think that sounds a marvellous solution,' said Louise. Throwing Rosie a keen glance, she added, 'Don't you, Rosie?'

'Yeah, I guess,' Rosie muttered, 'just as long as they don't keep on. They will,' she said when she caught sight of Louise's expression, 'just like they used to when I was at home. About everything—what I wore, where I went, who I saw, nagging all the time. And now I've got Skye it'll be worse—they'll go on about her as well. Is she too hot, or too cold? They'll probably drive me silly in the end.'

'It's only because they love you, Rosie,' said Louise, handing her a couple of paper towels on which to dry her hands. 'You'll feel the same about Skye—'

'I hope not,' said Rosie fiercely. 'I want Skye to be free—like a bird.'

Together they entered the ward and as Rosie made her way to Skye's incubator, Louise paused beside Oliver, where Elaine was tending the baby.

'Is everything all right, Elaine?' she asked.

'I'm not sure.' Elaine stared down at Oliver. 'He seems rather listless.'

'He was all right when the doctors came round, wasn't he?' asked Louise, opening the lid of the incubator and gently, so as not to disturb the many tubes, lifting Oliver out.

'Yes, he appeared to be,' Elaine replied. 'At least, the doctors seemed satisfied with him. Dr Miskin saw him and Dr Rawlings. But it's been since then…'

'Has his mum been in yet today?' asked Louise as she cradled the baby in both hands.

'No, not yet. It's probably nothing…'

'I'll phone a doctor, just to make sure,' said Louise,

gently stroking the baby's cheek with the back of her finger. 'It's better to be safe than sorry with these little ones.'

'Oh, here's Tracey now,' said Elaine.

Tracey Barrett hurried down the ward, her smile dissolving as she saw the two nurses with her son. 'What is it?' she asked anxiously. 'Is there anything wrong?'

'I don't think so,' Louise replied reassuringly, 'but he's been a little listless so I'm going to get a doctor to take a look at him. Look, you take him for a moment, Tracey. Probably all he needs is a cuddle from his mum.' Carefully she handed the baby to Tracey who sat down on the chair beside the incubator.

'I'll go and phone the doctor now,' said Louise. 'Two minutes, Elaine, then back into his cot.'

'It's like being on a roller-coaster every day,' Louise heard Tracey say to Elaine as she moved away. 'One day you're on top of the world because everything seems to be going so well then the next it's all worry and anxiety again.'

Louise went back to her office where she dialled the number for the paediatric doctors. Matt answered on the fourth ring. Involuntarily her grip tightened on the receiver. She hadn't seen him since Sunday morning and he hadn't been with the other doctors that morning when they had done their rounds.

'Matt, it's Louise,' she said, trying to keep her voice brisk and professional.

'Hello, Louise.' The tone of his voice changed slightly became more…more intimate.

'Matt.' She tried to ignore it, carrying straight on, 'I wonder if someone could come along, please. Oliver Barrett appears rather listless again. His observations are all right but Elaine was a bit concerned about him. I think

I'd like someone to check him out. Shara Miskin and Sandie saw him this morning during rounds.'

'OK,' said Matt, 'leave it with me. One of us will be along shortly.'

'Thanks.'

Quickly she replaced the receiver, thinking he might have said something about the weekend and not sure at that moment that she could cope with it. Her mind had been in turmoil for the past three days as she had battled to try to come to terms with her feelings and yet, if anyone had asked her, she knew she would still be hard put to say exactly how she felt.

It had been all very well to indulge in a bit of light-hearted fantasy on Michelle's wedding day, dreaming of how it could, even should have been for Matt and herself, and even the night she had spent with Matt, in spite of the unexpected surge of passion in their need for each other, could be put down to a self-indulgent wallowing in nostalgia, but the harsh reality was very different. For the stark facts were that they were but a stone's throw from the divorce courts and the process that would end their marriage once and for all. Why, even now, she thought as she busied herself with some of the never-ending tasks that constantly demanded her attention, Matt had probably instructed his solicitor. Wait until after the wedding, he had said. Well, the wedding was over now so there was no further need to delay.

So why did she feel so wretched? It was what she wanted, wasn't it? She knew it had to end, that it was inevitable that it should do so, because it should never have happened in the first place, because at the time it had been something that neither of them had really wanted.

But could they make it work now? Louise settled down to some paperwork but, try as she might to concentrate, the words of the marriage service kept coming back to haunt her.... 'For better, for worse...till death us do part...' Did that mean you kept trying, whatever life chucked at you? Was there any chance that she and Matt could start again, could put the past behind them and move on together? But surely that couldn't happen? Matt had never wanted to be married in the first place...and really, if she was truly honest, neither had she.

But...but they *were* married, a little voice persisted at the back of her mind. Yes, she told herself firmly, but that had been for a reason and that reason no longer existed...

'Louise.' Roma suddenly popped her head around the office door and made Louise jump. 'Dr Forrester is here. Oh...' She paused, staring at Louise in concern. 'Are you all right?'

'Yes.' Louise struggled to her feet. 'Yes, Roma, I'm fine, thanks. I'll come with you now.'

Her heart leapt when she caught sight of Matt. When he turned from examining Baby Oliver and his eyes met hers it was as if he knew exactly what her thoughts had been, as if he too had had the same thoughts. Which was ridiculous when she thought about it because while Matt, no doubt, was also ready to move on, it would be alone. If the weekend had affected him in any way it would simply have been because he'd enjoyed the wedding—the food, the drink, the company, the dancing—and as for what had followed, well, he'd never made any secret of the fact that he enjoyed sex.

'I don't think we have too much of a problem,' said Matt, looking down at Oliver, 'but I've just told Tracey we're going to run a few tests again. This may be a recurrence of his infection which does sometimes happen, and if that's the case we may need to give a further course of antibiotics and do some kidney X-rays.'

'Oh, no.' Tracey's hand flew to her mouth.

'Don't worry, Tracey,' said Louise quickly. 'It might not even be that. We'll get the tests done and go from there.' She glanced up as she spoke and through the glass partition saw that Nicky was talking to a young couple who had apparently just arrived on the ward. 'Would you excuse me a minute?' she said, and, as she left Tracey with Elaine, Matt joined her and together they walked out of the ward.

'Are you all right?' he murmured just loud enough so that only she heard.

'Yes, I'm fine,' she replied lightly.

'You don't look fine—you look, well, tired.'

'Thanks, Matt.' She pulled a face. 'That's all a girl needs to make her feel good.'

'Sorry.' He grinned. 'It's just that I know you've had quite a lot on recently, what with the job and the house and then the wedding and, well, I care about you.'

'Do you, Matt?' Turning slightly, she looked him straight in the eye.

'Yes,' he replied. 'Yes, of course I do.' Then softly, he said, 'Louise, I've been thinking, after the weekend and what happened, I really do think we need to talk.'

Squarely she continued to meet his gaze. 'What about?'

'Well, about everything really. Our future for a start…'

'I thought our future was already cut and dried,' she replied coolly.

'Well, yes, that's what I thought, but—'

'Matt, we can't talk now,' she interrupted him, 'not here. I have people waiting for me.' By this time they had reached the relatives' room into which Nicky was showing the young couple who had come to view the book of remembrance.

At this point Matt would have moved on, especially as

Mike Collard had also just arrived and joined the group, but instead he paused and looked at the couple who had a baby with them, a little girl of about a year old, carried by her father. 'Hello,' he said. 'It's Kevin and Teresa, isn't it?' As the woman nodded he gently touched the hand of their child. 'And this must be Sophie. I was present at this young lady's birth—I seem to remember she gave us all cause for concern at the time but, my, what a little beauty she's turned out to be.'

'Hello, Dr Forrester,' said Teresa. 'I didn't know you were back at Ellie's.'

'I've not been back long,' Matt replied.

'We've come to see the book of remembrance,' said Kevin. 'It's two years ago today that Justin died.'

'I'll come with you if I may,' said Matt quietly.

In silence they followed Mike Collard as he led the way to the quiet area beyond the relatives' room where, on the small altar, between the candles which he had already lit, he had placed the book of remembrance which listed the names of babies who had been on the special care baby unit at Ellie's and who had lost their battles for life.

The area was only small and Louise found herself standing very close to Matt as Kevin and Teresa, amidst their tears, viewed the book and placed a posy of flowers. Mike said some prayers and spoke a few words of comfort, and it was then that it happened. It started as a feeling of sadness in the pit of her stomach, sadness for the baby who had died and for his parents. That was where it usually ended for this, unfortunately, was an aspect that went with her job, something which every member of staff on the unit had to learn to cope with and to move on from.

And usually Louise did, but for some reason today she found herself unable to cope. The sadness rose from her stomach in a great wave that suddenly threatened to overwhelm her completely. She had no idea what had caused it, whether it was anything to do with the weekend, Michelle's wedding or what had followed with Matt, but quite suddenly tears were coursing down her cheeks and she was overwhelmed with sadness. Sadness certainly for the baby that they were remembering that day, but in addition to that the truth suddenly hit her that it was also grief for her own baby, the baby that she and Matt had lost.

Blindly she turned, briefly saw Matt's expression, which echoed her own, before his arms went round her to steady her and quietly he led her away.

CHAPTER TWELVE

IT WAS as if the floodgates had opened, releasing the torrent of pent-up sorrow and grief that Louise had suppressed since she'd suffered the loss of her own baby eighteen months before. Luckily her shift was almost over and somehow she had been able to hand over to her colleague before going off duty. In spite of her protests, Matt had insisted on driving her home, where together they spent the rest of that day grieving and talking about the child they had lost.

'This should have happened at the time,' said Matt once as he held her and comforted her.

'I know,' Louise agreed, 'but at the time I just seemed numb. I hardly felt anything and all I wanted to do was to put the whole thing behind me and get on with my life...and my career. I thought if I threw myself into work everything would be all right.'

'I begged you to go for some counselling,' said Matt.

'I know you did.' Louise nodded. 'But I didn't want to. It would be the first thing I would tell my patients to do...but I didn't think I needed it...'

'These emotions always come out somewhere down the line.' Gently Matt smoothed the hair back from her forehead.

'I should have gone, I see that now. Counselling would probably have released these feelings much earlier...' Louise paused to wipe her eyes and blow her nose. 'I wanted that baby, Matt,' she went on at last, 'I wanted it so much...'

'I know,' he said, his voice husky and charged with emotion, 'I know you did.'

'I didn't at first,' she went on, 'not when I first knew I was pregnant. I was pretty terrified then, but later, once we'd got used to the idea, I was really looking forward to it.'

'I know,' he said again, softly this time, his arm tightening around her, 'I know you were and, believe it or not, so was I.'

'Were you?' She turned her head to look at him as he sat beside her on the sofa. 'Were you really?'

'Of course I was. This was my child as well, you know.'

'I know, Matt, I'm sorry…' Her tears began to flow afresh and she reached for another tissue from the box Matt had thoughtfully placed on the coffee-table in front of them.

'Like you,' he went on after a moment, 'I was pretty devastated when you told me you were pregnant. At that time it was the last thing I wanted, what with my career training and everything, but also, like you, once I'd faced up to my responsibilities and got on with things I found myself getting quite excited at the prospect of being a father. And then, when it didn't happen, when I realised it wasn't to be…well, I don't know how I felt.'

'Trapped,' gulped Louise.

'Trapped?' Matt frowned. 'I wouldn't say I felt trapped exactly.'

'All right, resentful, then, because of the delay in your training…because we did only get married because I was pregnant, didn't we?' Louise went on. 'After all, we had both previously said that neither of us was ready for marriage or for children…'

'That's true,' Matt agreed quietly. 'I guess we did say that, but everything changed, Louise, and we were faced with a whole new set of circumstances. We'd had our pleasure and we were left with responsibilities to face up to...'

'Was that all it was for you—pleasure? A bit of fun?' she said slowly.

'At the time, probably, yes,' Matt agreed, 'but wasn't that what it was for you as well?'

'I suppose so,' she found herself admitting reluctantly. After all, wasn't that exactly what it had been for both of them? Their dates together—that weekend in Brighton? Hadn't it all been fun and excitement?

'The thing is,' Matt went on, 'there was no knowing where it would have led if you hadn't got pregnant when you did. I've asked myself that many times and I think we may well have continued to see each other—that was certainly what I wanted—and who knows? We could have ended up together anyway.'

'Married, you mean?' Louise stared at him.

'Possibly.' He gave a slight shrug. 'Who knows?'

'It's something we'll never know,' said Louise slowly. 'All I do know is that we married because a child was on the way and once that baby was no longer there our marriage fell apart.'

They were silent after that, each reflecting on those difficult months after Louise had lost the baby and they had seemed to grow further and further apart.

At last, with a deep sigh, Matt stood up. 'I have to go,' he said. 'I must go back to the hospital and make up some lost time. Are you sure you'll be all right?' he said anxiously, looking down at her. 'I could arrange for someone to come and be with you.'

'No, I'll be all right,' she replied quickly, 'Really,' she added, catching sight of his dubious expression. 'In fact, I'd quite like some time on my own.'

'All right.' He nodded. 'If you're sure. But I'll be back later.'

She opened her mouth to argue, to protest, but his expression put paid to that and suddenly she found the fact that he intended coming back quite comforting. After he'd gone she cried some more then, exhausted by the events of the day, she slept.

True to his word, Matt did come back, bringing food with him which Louise didn't really want but which she ate a little of to please him. And when he insisted on staying she had very little energy to protest and found that really she didn't want him to go anyway.

'I intend to be here with you, at least for the time being,' he said. 'Delayed grief can be very traumatic and I don't want you facing it alone.'

Once she was in bed in the smaller spare room where she had slept since Matt had left, she heard him come up the stairs and go into the main bedroom. Neither of them had made any reference to the night they had spent together after Michelle's and Andy's wedding when they had both slept in the bed they had once shared.

It was comforting to have him in the house at this time when her emotions felt so raw, even though she knew it wouldn't last, that it was just a temporary arrangement. In time, presumably, they would continue with their original plan that would lead to the sale of their house and their divorce.

At Matt's insistence she took some time off work, spending her days in and around the house enjoying leisurely lie-ins, breakfasts on her balcony, walks along the riverbank, a couple of shopping trips into town and the occasional lunch at Angelo's. And throughout it all Matt was there in the background of her days—joining her whenever he was off duty in whatever she had planned for that day, or, on the days he was working, hurrying home so that they could share a meal together.

It was a strange, slightly unreal but pleasant time and gradually Louise felt herself coming to terms with all that had happened.

Almost before she knew it, Michelle and Andy were back from their honeymoon, and as soon as Michelle heard that Louise had been off work she rushed over to the house to see her.

'Lou!' she cried when Louise opened the door. 'What's happened? Are you ill?'

'Michelle, come in.' Louise hugged her friend. 'It's lovely to see you. Wow, look at that tan! What was it like? Did you have a wonderful time?'

'It was glorious,' said Michelle with a sigh as Louise stood aside and she brushed past her in the tiny hallway. 'All white beaches, blue skies and waving palms.'

'Sounds like heaven,' said Louise.

'It was,' said Michelle, 'and Andy wasn't so bad either,' she added with a grin.

'Come through. I was sitting in the garden. Would you like some lemonade?'

'Please.' Michelle followed Louise into the kitchen where she poured a glass of the lemonade she had made that morning, then they made their way into the garden and sat down in the chairs positioned around a table on the wooden decking.

'Right,' said Michelle, taking a mouthful of her lemonade, 'I want to know what this is all about.'

'There's not really a lot to tell,' said Louise with a little shrug.

'Well, that's a matter of opinion—you look decidedly

peaky. Whatever is it, Lou? I don't think I've ever known you to be ill.'

'Well, I wouldn't say I was ill exactly.'

'So what is it?' Are you on sick leave?'

'I took a few days off sick,' Louise admitted, 'and since then I've had a few annual leave days and just been thoroughly lazy.'

'So what were the sick days for?' Michelle set her glass down on the table and frowned at Louise.

'It's a bit of a long story really, but basically I suppose you could call it delayed grief or something like that.'

'Delayed grief…' Michelle stared at her. 'You don't mean…?'

'Yes,' Louise said, then sighed. 'I mean exactly that.'

'Oh, Lou.' Michelle continued to stare helplessly at her for a long moment then, rising to her feet, she moved round the table, put her arms around her friend and hugged her wordlessly. 'If I'm honest,' she said at last, moving away and back to her chair, 'I'm not really surprised. I always thought at the time that you got over it far too quickly.'

'Yes, well, my answer was to put it to the back of my mind and buckle down to work. I can see now it was the worst thing I could have done—I even shut Matt out in the process. But there you are, it happened…and I guess in the last few days it all caught up with me.'

'Do you know what triggered it?' asked Michelle curiously.

'I've been thinking about that,' Louise replied, 'and I've come to the conclusion it was a combination of several things. I think it was partly Matt coming back again, seeing him, remembering how it had once been…then there was your wedding and that seemed to stir up all sorts of emotions, but the final straw was when a couple came onto the ward the other day to view the book of remembrance because it was the two-year anniversary of the child they had lost. They had their new baby with them and Matt was there because he had been present at this baby's birth and...I don't know, suddenly I found myself in tears, which was ridiculous really because that wasn't the first time I've had to deal with something like that, but for some reason once I started crying I wasn't able to stop. And I seemed to have cried ever since...'

'Well, that's good.' Michelle nodded. 'Best thing that could have happened, in my opinion.' She was silent for a moment and in the quietness all they could hear was the song of a blackbird in bushes nearby and the distant hum of a boat on the river. Then she said, 'You say this couple had another baby?'

'Yes, a little girl.'

'Which, of course, is the best possible solution.'

'I know, Michelle, but that's hardly going to happen in my case, is it?'

'Maybe not.' Michelle shrugged. 'At least, not at the present time. But they didn't say there was any reason why you couldn't have more children, did they?'

Louise shook her head. 'No, they said what happened was just one of those things, nature's way of taking care of something that wasn't meant to be.'

They fell silent again then Michelle looked up curiously and said, 'How has Matt been in all this?'

'Actually, I have to say,' said Louise softly, 'he's been fantastic.'

'Well, that's no more than I would have expected—he's a fantastic guy, Lou.'

'Yes, I guess. I know,' she added helplessly. 'He's hardly left my side since it happened—only to go to work, of course.'

Michelle stared at her. 'You mean...' she glanced over her shoulder into the house as if she expected Matt to suddenly materialise '...he's staying here?'

'Yes,' Louise said. 'He was absolutely adamant.'

'Well, good for him.' Michelle took another sip of her lemonade and as she set the glass down she threw Louise a glance. 'So...tell me,' she began hesitantly, 'is there any chance...I mean, do you think you and he...?'

'Go on, spit it out,' said Louise with a sudden laugh. 'What you really want to know is if there's a chance we are going to get back together again, is that it?'

'Well, yes, I suppose it is,' Michelle said eagerly.

'If you'd asked me that question a couple of weeks ago I would have said, no, definitely not, no chance...'

'And now?' demanded Michelle, her eyes wide with anticipation.

'Now? Well, now I'm not so sure,' Louise admitted at last.

'That's definitely an improvement,' said Michelle firmly.

'I don't know that anything is going to come of it,' said Louise, 'but we have talked, talked endlessly really, about everything—about losing the baby, of course, about how we felt about that, even about what might have happened between us if we hadn't got married when we did.'

'And what conclusion did you reach over that?' asked Michelle.

Louise took a deep breath. 'We found ourselves thinking that it might have happened anyway, even though it would have been further down the line. The thing is, Michelle, I thought that Matt felt trapped after I lost the baby. But he says, no, it wasn't that way at all and, in fact, he was also grieving but was afraid to show it for fear of upsetting me. He also felt I shut him out at that time, and I suppose, if

I'm honest, I did. You see, I thought he only married me because of the baby, and when there was no baby I assumed he bitterly regretted what he had done. And now I gather he felt the same—that I only married him because I was pregnant and afterwards wished I hadn't. Things got bad between us and when the opportunity came up for him to go to Scotland he took it because he thought we both needed space.'

'So, let me get this straight,' said Michelle when she had finished. 'Are you now living together in the strict sense of the word?'

Louise hesitated. 'Not really,' she said at last. 'Matt is sleeping in the main room and I'm in my little room...apart from...' She trailed off, afraid she'd said too much and hoping Michelle wouldn't notice.

'Apart from what?' Michelle demanded.

'Oh, nothing really.' She tried to dismiss it.

'No. Go on, what did you mean—apart from what?' Michelle obviously wasn't going to let it go.

'Apart from your wedding night...'

'My wedding night?' Michelle's eyes widened. 'What about my wedding night?'

'We came back here after you'd gone, that's all,' said Louise with a little shrug.

'And...?' prompted Michelle.

'And we slept together. It was probably the champagne that did it...and...and the day. Everything really,' she said, her eyes filling with sudden tears. 'The service...the flowers...the music...'

'So what was it like?' asked Michelle softly. 'I know what my wedding night was like for me, but what was it like for you?'

'Wonderful,' said Louise, wiping away her tears with

the back of her hand as they trickled down her cheeks. 'Just wonderful.'

Michelle gave a deep sigh and they sat on together in the warm afternoon sunshine. What Louise didn't tell Michelle, however, was that it hadn't only been on her wedding night that she and Matt had slept together.

Two nights previously there had been a thunderstorm. Louise hated thunderstorms. She had put up with the flashes of lightning and booming thunder for as long as she could but when one particularly loud crack of thunder had sounded directly overhead, she had jumped out of her bed and run into Matt's room. He had been sitting up in bed and as she'd come into the room he'd lifted back the covers for her to join him.

'What kept you?' He'd smiled as she'd slipped into bed beside him. 'I expected you half an hour ago.'

And the next night, even though there had been no sign of a storm, somehow it had simply been taken for granted that they would sleep together.

In the end Louise was pleased to return to work, to her busy unit, to her staff and to those special babies entrusted to her care. She found that in her absence five new babies had come onto the unit, Beth Cleaver was almost ready to go home, Gabrielle Fox was continuing to improve, as was Skye Bradley, while Oliver Barrett was unfortunately still beset by problems, especially urinary tract infections, but he was battling bravely and Neil Richardson was optimistic about his progress.

On the second day Louise was back on the unit she and Matt arranged to meet each other in the staff canteen for lunch, but when the time came Louise found herself delayed in a meeting with social workers about one of the new babies on the unit who was at the centre of domestic turmoil. By the time the meeting was over she feared that Matt would probably have had to go back to Paediatrics, unable to wait.

'I must fly,' she said to Nicky, who looked set to waylay her. 'I'm supposed to be meeting Matt and I'm already about half an hour late.'

'He's in great demand today,' said Nicky.

'What do you mean?' Louise paused, one hand on the door handle.

'There was a woman looking for him just now,' Nicky replied. 'I sent her down to Paediatrics.'

'Who was it?' At this point she was only idly curious imagining it to be a patient or a relative or maybe a member of staff from another department.

'Don't know.' Nicky shrugged. 'Never seen her before. I think she said her name was Serena something or other. She had a strong Scottish accent.'

Louise had been about to let herself out of the unit but at Nicky's words she stopped dead. Serena. In the last few weeks she'd forgotten all about Serena.

'Are you all right, Louise?'

She turned sharply and found Nicky staring at her curiously. 'Yes,' she said quickly, 'I'm fine.'

'You looked as if you'd seen a ghost,' said Nicky lightly.

'No, I'm OK. But, like I say, I'd better go.'

Quickly but with a certain amount of apprehension she made her way down to the staff canteen. Serena had been the woman Matt had worked with in Scotland, the woman who had invited him to spend Christmas at her family home. That was all she herself knew about her, but had that been all there was to know? Had Serena meant more to Matt than Louise had realised? And if she hadn't, what had brought her all the way down from Edinburgh to Sussex to see him again?

She caught sight of Matt as soon as she entered the canteen. Still wearing his white coat, he was sitting at a table in the window while opposite him was an extremely attractive woman with a mass of auburn hair dressed in a tailored black suit. Her hands were in front of her on the table, and even as Louise paused in the entrance and watched, Matt leaned forward and covered the woman's hands with his own, at the same time staring into her face and talking intently to her.

In a sudden wave of nausea Louise turned away and hurried from the building.

Louise didn't see Matt again before she went off duty, and after she'd handed over to the incoming staff she drove home and let herself into the house, her thoughts in turmoil.

Had she been a fool, imagining that she and Matt might have been on the brink of reconciliation? She wasn't even sure in her own mind that she had been thinking on those lines, at least not until Michelle had come to visit her and she had found herself talking about how she and Matt seemed to have been working through their problems. And it had seemed that way to her, especially during the time she had been away from work and Matt had been so extraordinarily kind to her. But was that all it had been, kindness and pity? Her heart sank at the thought. She didn't want his pity—she didn't want anyone's pity. But hadn't they sorted out all that business about feeling trapped by marriage and losing the baby and about how they had felt?

Maybe that was it, she thought with a little jolt as she walked into the kitchen and filled the kettle. Maybe all they had sorted out was how they had felt then—in the past. It was the present that was important now, and what was to happen in the future. Perhaps Matt had moved on; maybe during that year of their separation he had met someone else and had only come back to finalise things between them and tie up any loose ends. What if he and this woman Serena had fallen in love and were now an item and she was simply waiting for him to go back to her?

Louise stared out of the window without really seeing what she was looking at. Surely that couldn't be the case? Matt had slept with her—several times now since he'd been back. Surely he wouldn't have instigated that if he was in love with someone else? And it had been him who had instigated it, hadn't it?

She turned away from the window as a sudden rush of uncertainty hit her. The night of the wedding she could hardly remember—that had probably been a mixture of champagne and old times' sake, but on the night of the storm it had been she who had crept into bed with him, not the other way round, and what of last night? Slowly it dawned on her that she had gone to him, simply taking it for granted that this was what would happen.

But it had been good, very good, every bit as good as it had been all that time ago at the very beginning of their relationship and at the start of their marriage. And it wasn't only the sex. Satisfying and fantastic as that was, it was having him there beside her at work, and in the house, sharing every aspect of their lives, even seemingly trivial domestic matters.

The torment went on, and that's what it was because in those hours while she waited for Matt to come home Louise finally recognised that she was still in love with her husband and always had been. But was it all now too late? Had she found him only to lose him again?

By the time Louise heard the sound of Matt's key in the lock she was in a state of anxiety, and it must have been evident for as he came into the living room and greeted her he threw her a second keen glance. 'Are you all right?' he said.

'Yes,' she replied quickly. 'A bit tired,' she added.

'I was worried,' he said. 'You didn't come for lunch.'

'I got caught in a meeting,' she replied, then found herself holding her breath as he set his briefcase down and took off his jacket. Would he tell her about Serena? And if he did, could she bear it?

'It was a shame you couldn't make it,' he said as he followed her into the kitchen. 'I had a visitor, someone I would have liked you to meet.'

'Really?' She hoped she sounded casual but feared her voice had come out as a high-pitched squeak.

'Yes,' he went on, 'it was Serena—Serena Stewart. Do you remember me mentioning her before?'

She nodded, amazed by how much it hurt just to even think about it. 'Wasn't she the one you spent Christmas with?' she managed to say at last.

'Yes, that's right.' He gave a sudden chuckle. 'It was all pretty grim really.'

'You didn't say that before,' said Louise. 'You implied it was very pleasant.'

'Did I?' He frowned. 'Well, I guess I didn't want to sound ungrateful. After all, she'd only invited me because she felt sorry for me...'

'Because you were on your own—yes, you said,' she added sharply.

'Yes, well.' He threw her a quick glance, obviously surprised by her tone. 'Like I say, she felt sorry for me and I felt sorry for her so we must have been a pretty drippy pair.'

'Why did you feel sorry for her?' Suddenly, in spite of herself, Louise needed to know.

'Because she'd just split up with her boyfriend.'

'Oh, I see.' She stared at him. 'So,' she went on coolly after a moment, 'the pair of you were commiserating with each other all over Christmas—sounds pretty cosy.'

'It wasn't quite like that.' Matt pulled a face. 'For a start, her father was a very dour character, her brothers were a little too fond of their drink and on Boxing Day afternoon her ex-boyfriend turned up, demanding to know who the hell I was.'

'So what happened?'

'Luckily, I managed to persuade him that I was simply a colleague of Serena's. I left the next morning. In the end I was glad to get back to the hospital,' he added ruefully.

'What is she doing in Franchester?' Louise frowned.

'She was on her way to Southampton for a family funeral,' Matt replied. 'She took a detour to come and see me—she wanted to tell me that she and her boyfriend are getting married in the summer.'

For a moment Louise didn't know what to say and she simply stared at Matt.

'It was great really,' he went on after a moment, blissfully unaware at the turmoil that his friend's visit had caused, 'because she also wanted to know how things had worked out for me.'

There was silence between them for a long moment then in a small voice Louise heard herself say, 'And what did you tell her?'

'I told her that when I first came back I really didn't think there was very much hope but that gradually, as time has gone on, I've realised that I never stopped loving you, that, in fact, I love you more today than I ever have and that the last couple of weeks have given me reason to hope that we can get our marriage back on track.'

'You told her all that?' whispered Louise, staring at him.

'Shouldn't I have done?' he said gently.

'It's just that...I thought... Oh, it doesn't really matter what I thought.'

'Yes, it does. Go on, tell me. I want to know.'

'Well, it's just that... I saw you in the canteen with...with Serena.'

'Did you?' He looked surprised. 'Why didn't you come over? I wanted her to meet you.'

'Did you?'

'Yes, of course I did. I told you...' He trailed off. 'Why didn't you, Louise?' he asked quietly at last.

'Because...I thought you and she might be an item,' she admitted at last.

'Me and Serena?' There was amazement in Matt's voice now.

'Is that so surprising?' she said. 'All I knew was that you had worked with her for the past year, that you had spent Christmas together—which can be an emotional time whatever the circumstances—and that she had turned up here to see you, miles away from her home town. She also, from what I could see, looked very attractive...and the pair of you seemed, well, comfortable together, to say the least.' She shrugged. 'So, really, what was I to think?'

'But what about us? Hasn't it meant anything to you that we've become close again in the last few weeks?' he asked with soft incredulity.

'Of course it has,' she whispered. 'Of course it has, Matt,' she added helplessly, 'but it didn't alter the fact that for a moment there I thought that you and she may have come to mean something to each other...'

'And would it have bothered you if we had?' he said softly.

'Oh, yes,' she whispered as she stepped into the warm comforting circle of his arms. 'Yes, it would, most definitely it would.'

EPILOGUE

THE clematis was in bloom once again, tumbling gloriously over the pergola. To Louise it hardly seemed possible that over a year had passed since she and Michelle had sat there on the wooden decking, sipping home-made lemonade and discussing Michelle's honeymoon and the rather precarious state of her own marriage.

So much had happened in that year that at times it seemed she was scarcely able to take it all in. It had started, of course, with she and Matt deciding to have another attempt at making their marriage work—the visit to their respective solicitors had been abandoned and it had been agreed that their little house by the river most definitely wasn't for sale.

The long hot summer had passed in a glorious haze as together they'd made up for all the time they'd lost.

'We must have been mad,' Matt said to her one morning after they had made love and were lying together in one another's arms. 'I can't believe now that I walked away from you.'

'And I can't believe I let you,' she answered with a little sigh.

The cream roses were still in bloom when they asked Mike Collard if he would conduct a simple blessing ceremony on their marriage at his local church. He had been delighted to oblige and they had asked Louise's parents and her brother and his family, Matt's two sisters and their families, Michelle and Andy and several other friends, including colleagues from Ellie's and Angelo and Maria to bear witness as they reaffirmed their wedding vows. Afterwards, they all came back to the little house by the river and sat outside beneath the pergola, sipping champagne and nibbling delicacies provided by Maria.

It was quite still in the garden now, without as much as a breath of wind, and as Louise stood there, breathing in the scent of the soft, damp earth, she wanted to continue with her daydream to think about the second honeymoon they had enjoyed in Venice, but at that moment outside in the street she heard a car door slam. She turned, went back into the house and was just in time to see Matt come into the hall.

'Hello,' she said, moving forward and lifting her face for his kiss. 'I wasn't expecting you home this lunchtime.'

'I know.' He grinned sheepishly. 'I'm not really meant to be here, but somehow I find it difficult to stay away. I wondered if you were all right.'

'I'm fine,' she said with a little laugh. 'Didn't you think I'd be able to cope on my own?'

'Of course I did. I have no doubts about the ability of Sister Forrester. After all, she's had plenty of practice.' He paused. 'Speaking of which, I saw Joe Barrett this morning—he was carrying out some repairs at the hospital for the firm he works for. He asked to be remembered to you.'

'That's nice,' said Louise. 'Did you ask how Oliver is?'

'Of course,' Matt replied, as he followed her up the stairs and into the first-floor sitting room. 'He's thriving, apparently. Trying to pull himself up. Joe says he thinks he'll be walking soon.'

'Well, that's wonderful.' Louise smiled. 'When you think of all the problems he had. And Tracey, how is she?'

'Ah,' said Matt, 'I was coming to her. Joe says she's just found out that she's pregnant again. Needless to say, they're delighted.'

'Yes,' replied Louise, 'they would be.' Taking Matt's hand, she led him across the room to the cradle that stood in front of the French windows.

'How's he been?' whispered Matt, gazing down at the baby who slept peacefully, his head with its soft dark hair turned to one side.

'You've only been gone four hours,' said Louise with a chuckle. 'He's been fine. Really, he has.'

'Harry,' Matt said proudly, with more than a hint of wonder in his voice, 'Harry Forrester. You know, sometimes I can still hardly believe it. That he's really here, and that he is ours.'

'I know,' said Louise softly. 'It's pretty awesome, isn't it?'

Her pregnancy had not been without its anxieties, which was natural, given her history, but once they had passed what had become in their minds the danger point they had relaxed somewhat, and Louise had found that she'd actually enjoyed the final months. Matt had been by her side when their son Harry had been born, and had shared with her that wonderful moment of bonding when he'd been placed in her arms. And ever since, Matt had been reluctant to leave her side until that very morning when he had finally been forced to return to work.

'Mike phoned earlier,' she said, as they both continued to gaze at their son. 'He's coming over this evening to see Harry and to talk about the christening.'

'That's nice,' said Matt. As the baby stirred, he said, 'He's waking up. Good. I'll be able to have a cuddle before I go back to work.' Reaching into the cradle, he lifted the baby gently in his hands. 'Isn't he perfect?' he murmured, as he studied the tiny features and the soft wisps of dark hair.

'Yes,' Louise agreed softly, 'quite perfect.'

'Just like his mum,' said Matt. Leaning across the baby, gently he kissed her mouth. 'Thank you,' he murmured.

'What for?' she asked.

'For being my wife,' he said, 'and for being Harry's mum, but most of all simply for being you.'

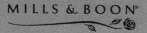

MILLS & BOON

Medical Romance™

DAISY AND THE DOCTOR *by Meredith Webber*

Dr Julian Austin doesn't believe in love – so psychologist Daisy is his perfect bride. She's been hurt too often to trust in love. Then Daisy realises that, for her, marriage to Julian would be exactly the love match she wants to avoid – and Julian starts to wonder – if love doesn't exist, what's happening to his heart?

THE SURGEON'S MARRIAGE *by Maggie Kingsley*

Doctors Tom and Helen Brooke have a great marriage – when they can find time to see each other. Despite being overworked and under-appreciated, Helen knows she and Tom have something special. Then a series of misunderstandings makes her think that Tom doesn't care – and Tom is faced with a fight to save his marriage...

THE MIDWIFE'S BABY WISH *by Gill Sanderson*

As Keldale's midwife, Lyn Pierce is kept busy! But when Dr Adam Fletcher joins the practice he awakens emotions she can't afford to let herself feel. For it soon becomes clear that Adam wants a family – and while Lyn can give him love, giving him the children he longs for is an impossible dream...

On sale 4th April 2003

Available at most branches of WH Smith, Tesco, Martins, Borders, Eason, Sainsbury's and all good paperback bookshops.

0303/03a

dark angel
LYNNE GRAHAM

Knight in shining armour
or avenging angel?

Available from 21st March 2003

*Available at most branches of WH Smith,
Tesco, Martins, Borders, Eason, Sainsbury's
and all good paperback bookshops.*

0403/135/MB68

Become a Panel Member

If YOU are a regular United Kingdom buyer of Mills & Boon®
Medical Romance™ you might like to tell us your opinion of the
books we publish to help us in publishing the books *you* like.

Mills & Boon have a Reader Panel of Medical Romance™ readers.
Each person on the panel receives a short questionnaire (taking
about five minutes to complete) every third month asking for
opinions of the past month's Medical Romances. All people who
send in their replies have a chance of winning a FREE year's supply
of Medical Romances.

If YOU would like to be considered for inclusion on the panel please
fill in and return the following survey. We can't guarantee that
everyone will be on the panel but first come will be first considered.

Where did you buy this novel?

❑   WH Smith
❑   Tesco
❑   Borders
❑   Sainsbury's
❑   Direct by mail
❑   Other (please state) _____

What themes do you enjoy most in the Mills & Boon® novels that
you read? (Choose all that apply.)

❑   Amnesia
❑   Family drama (including babies/young children)
❑   Hidden/Mistaken identity
❑   Historical setting
❑   Marriage of convenience
❑   Medical drama
❑   Mediterranean men
❑   Millionaire heroes
❑   Mock engagement or marriage
❑   Outback setting
❑   Revenge